Leaving Waverly

A PREQUEL NOVELLA

CRIPPLE CREEK SERIES

SARA R. TURNQUIST

MOUNTAIN
SUMMIT PRESS

If you would like to stay up-to-date on this and other series from Sara and receive a free ebook, sign up for her newsletter:

https://saraturnquist.com/list

For my readers.
You keep me going.

Chapter One

The sun shone bright on Lauren Crawford as she made her way across the field. A breeze pressed her skirts against legs that stretched out as swiftly as they could. Lifting her chin, she turned her face upward, eager for warmth. Mother would not approve.

"You'll freckle," she'd say.

Lauren didn't care. The sun was a fine companion on her daily walk to and from the plantation house.

So much had changed in the last two years. These fields were at one time teeming with slaves. Now everything was different. Not that she minded. Slavery seemed to go against the essence of polite society—barbaric and cruel. But the terrible practice had ended at a great cost to many. Unthinkable bloodshed...

Lauren pushed the memories aside. Best not to think on such things. No, there was no need to think on that.

Returning her gaze forward once again, she picked up speed. It would behoove her to not be late for dinner. Father might become suspicious. And that would lead to questions.

And she dared not let him discover where her midmorning strolls took her.

Moments later, she crossed a small stream. Stone by stone, she hopped over, holding her skirt. Mother would have enough to scold her for without a soaked hem.

A voice rang out and carried in the wind.

Who was that? Was someone hurt?

"Can anyone hear me?" It was a man's voice. Dare she follow it? Her mind warned against such a pursuit, telling of potential dangers.

"Help me!"

He sounded desperate. Was it a sharecropper? A farmer? One of her father's workers? Either way, she could not leave someone, even a stranger, to suffer. Perhaps she might approach in safety and keep her distance until she determined the circumstances. After all, she was within a few yards of the plantation house.

Moving toward the voice that was still calling for help, she climbed the sloped embankment and went further up another small hill. There, from the top, she saw a figure next to a fallen horse. What had happened?

The man scanned the area.

There was nowhere for her to hide.

As he looked in her direction, he called to her, "Please." He faced her, though the distance between them was great. She couldn't quite make out his features. "My horse is injured. I need help."

What was she to do? Perhaps she should run to fetch Father or one of the men who worked for him. But would the horse survive that long? What was the nature of the animal's injury?

Her heart beat hard. Maybe she should help this man now.

But what of her own safety?

Shaking her head, she pulled her things more tightly to her chest and marched forward. She could handle herself.

As she neared the man, kneeling by the horse, she could make out some of his more distinct characteristics, though he did not look her way again. He was young, not more than five years her senior. And he had dark hair, wavy, though it was cut short.

And...and the blood. Everywhere. On the young man, on the grass around the horse, and soaking the cloth the man pressed to the animal's leg.

Lauren swallowed hard against the sudden uneasiness in her stomach. One more step and the metallic smell slammed into her senses. Her hand flew to her mouth.

She could do this. She would. She had to.

The young man turned, and his deep brown eyes found hers. Brief relief registered among the surprise in his gaze. He frowned and looked back at the distressed mare, leaning onto her wound.

Shifting, the animal let out a pitiful noise.

Setting her things to the side, Lauren knelt beside him. "What happened?"

"She stepped in a hole. Her leg is broken." His voice shook as he spoke.

That wasn't all. The blood revealed as much.

Lauren was no stable master. Caring for horses was not her forte. Still, she knew something was seriously wrong.

With a boldness that surprised her, she reached forth and lifted the cloth, tugging at the young man's hand.

He relented and raised it.

The bone was visible, protruding through the skin.

She turned her head, hand pressed to her mouth, not able to control her gagging.

Several moments passed before her stomach calmed. Once she had control of herself, she faced him.

"She's not going to make it." Lauren kept her voice soft.

The young man shook his head, gaze fixed on the horse.

Lauren looked at the mare's face, then at the man's grimace. She laid a hand on his arm.

He was shaking. From the effort of holding the compress on? Or from emotion?

"She's in a lot of pain. You need to let her be at peace."

The man's eyes slid closed, and he turned his face into his shoulder opposite where Lauren sat.

When he lifted his head, Lauren expected him to argue, but he nodded.

Moving her hand down his arm to his hands, she pulled them off the wound.

He allowed it.

Then she helped him stand, keeping one hand on his arm, the other on his hands. "Do you have a gun?"

He nodded but didn't move.

"Where is it?"

Jerking his head toward the saddlebag, now several feet from the horse, he began to pull away.

She squeezed his arm. "I'll get it."

Lauren retrieved the bag and brought it to the young man. She had no desire to touch the weapon, and no knowledge of how to fire it.

Holding it out to him, she watched the shifting of his features as he opened the flap and pulled out a pistol. His brows furrowed, and he swallowed.

Setting the bag at their feet, she then nodded to him.

He stepped to the mare's head, crouching down. "You've been a good horse, old friend. I'm sorry." His voice caught.

Lauren's heart ached. How long had this animal been his companion? His friend? In the next moment, she stood beside him as he rose. She placed an arm on his shoulder.

He glanced at her, his eyes first catching, then gazing into hers. Did he seek the kind of comfort she wished she could give him?

The young man turned his focus to the horse and straightened his arm, aiming at the back of the mare's head.

Lauren held her breath.

Nothing happened.

The man's shoulder shook. Would he be able to do this? He had to. This animal was in distress. She hurt more every second that passed. And there was nothing they could do for her but to end it.

Lauren prayed for strength for the man.

He shook harder.

And Lauren's resolve strengthened.

She ran her hand down his arm to the pistol, covering his hand with her own, laying her finger over his on the trigger.

And pulled.

Clementine was dead.

The shot fired, and she was gone.

Was he grateful? Or sad?

The young lady removed her hand as Tom pulled the pistol back to himself, but he could not stop the shaking. It worsened.

But instead of moving away, the woman embraced him. "Hold onto me."

He did. Wrapping his arms around her, he held to her as if she were the only thing keeping him upright. Perhaps she was.

Clementine had been with him since he was a boy. They had grown together. She had been his constant companion and friend. There wasn't anything he couldn't tell her. And now she was gone. Just like that. Would anything be right again?

At length, the shaking did subside. Then he pulled back. Hazel eyes, warm and comforting, stared up at him.

"Thank you," he managed, face warming. How could he have fallen apart in front of this beautiful woman?

One glance at her appearance, he noted her refinement. Probably the plantation master's daughter. This would not go well for him.

"I apologize for any inconvenience, miss. I didn't mean to keep you." He averted his gaze.

"Keep me? It was better I was here to help. Do you need assistance getting home? Perhaps help with..." Her voice trailed.

He closed his eyes. Her unsaid words rang in his mind.

"No, thank you. I can manage. Maybe you best get home. I don't wish your father to worry after you."

"Nor I yours."

Tom met her gaze. "Are you so concerned after my wellbeing?"

She couldn't mean it. After all, this wasn't the first southern belle he had met.

"Of course." The woman jerked back as if stung.

Looking into her eyes, he wanted to believe her but found cause to doubt. He walked to the discarded saddlebag, pushing the gun inside. When he stood, slinging his burden over his shoulder, he found the young woman as she had been, eyes wide, mouth agape.

"Something the matter?"

She shut her mouth and crossed her arms. "No, of course not."

They squared off for some moments. What had happened here?

She let her arms fall. "I need to get home." Turning away, she stepped toward the pile of things she had dropped.

"Let me help you." His longer stride brought him to the

small stack before her. He crouched and gathered the books and slates.

She all but jerked them from his hands, pulling them to her chest.

He opened his mouth but then closed it. Far be it from him to wonder after the actions of these rich women.

As they stood, they faced each other in silence once more.

"Please, tell your father I will have my...horse off his property by nightfall."

Her eyes softened for a moment, and she nodded. Then she spun and walked in the opposite direction.

"And..." he called after her. Why did he do that?

She turned.

He looked away; his face heated. But he needed to say it. It was only right. So, he faced her once more. "Thank you."

She nodded and walked away.

It was likely he'd never see her again.

Tom walked to his father's homestead with mixed emotions. He had not intended to offend the young woman, only to speak the truth. Why did it bother her so? The ladies of society he'd come across were coy and flirtatious, only interested in ensnaring his good favor. For what, he did not know.

But this woman, she cared naught for the title nor for him it seemed. And that bothered him. Though it shouldn't. Perhaps he simply feared if it did not go well for him with the daughter, it might affect his dealings with the father. And he needed this tenancy.

There weren't many plantations in Waverly at which he could seek tenancy, and none so near to Pa's farm. This was the most ideal situation. Especially now with Clementine gone.

His heart fell. The loss still stung. Clementine had been a constant friend to him. Would there ever be another soul he could share his hopes and dreams with?

Not even Pa understood. But then, Pa was afraid for him. Could he not see that Tom's plans for the future were his best chance for happiness?

The family farm sat before him in the distance—a moderate and comfortable home at the far end of a small property alongside a barn. Fields of vegetables stretched out across the parcel of land.

Farming was hard work. It was long work. And Tom hated it with a passion.

But he did not despise everything about life on the farm. Running toward him at full speed were two reasons to love every minute of it: Jeremiah and Josephine.

They tackled him to the ground; but soon enough, he got the best of them.

"Tom Matthews, you better not be wrestling with your sister!"

It was Ma, yelling from the porch.

He looked over his shoulder at his mother's frame in the doorway. "Sorry, Ma!"

She shook her head and went back inside.

Jeremiah and Josephine laughed so hard they were grasping at their sides.

Tom stood and reached both of his hands down to help them to their feet.

Once everyone stood upright again, Josephine wrapped her arms around her big brother.

"Where's Clementine?" Jeremiah searched the horizon.

Tom sighed and fought down a wave of emotion. He needn't let the twins see the depth of his sadness.

Giving Jeremiah's hair a tousle, he shrugged. "Had to let her go."

"Where?" Jeremiah's voice squeaked and his hands flew to his mouth.

Josephine giggled and Jeremiah shot her a mean look.

Tom found reason to smile at that, remembering his own transition into manhood.

"Clementine got hurt. And no one could help her. She was suffering. So, I told her it was okay if she went to heaven."

Jeremiah made a face.

Josephine grimaced.

Did they realize what he had done?

Josephine hugged him tighter.

He let her, enclosing her with an arm.

Jeremiah's gaze fell to the ground. "What are you going to do now?"

"I'll just have to work extra hard and earn more money to get another horse." The words felt wrong.

"Does that mean you won't leave?" Josephine's green eyes met his.

Tom took in a deep breath and let it out. "No. I have to go."

Jeremiah shook his head and crossed his arms in front of his chest, kicking at a rock in the path.

They didn't understand. How could he expect them to? All they knew was that their big brother would go away some day. He couldn't seem to explain that he couldn't breathe here. Not anymore. Not after the war. Not after what happened to Otis.

"Don't be sad," Josephine touched his arm.

Tom shook his head. "I'm not. Just thinking."

When Josephine looked up at him, her eyes had that same depth Ma's did sometimes.

"Guess who I met today?" Tom picked up his step toward the house.

Josephine and Jeremiah walked alongside him.

"Who?" Jeremiah's interest was piqued.

But it was not Jeremiah who would find this tidbit most intriguing.

"The plantation master's daughter."

"Really?" Josephine all but squealed. "A real southern belle?"

Tom nodded.

"Was she beautiful?"

"She was. Hair the color of the smoothest chocolate, eyes of cinnamon."

"Someone's hungry." Jeremiah rolled his eyes.

"And her dress? Was it grand?" Josephine held her folded hands by her cheek.

"Much too fussy. Your dresses are far more practical. I would rather be with you any day of the week."

Josephine gave him her biggest smile. "You only say that because you're my brother. You have to."

"I say it because it's true." Tom reached for the latch and pushed the door open.

They were welcomed with the pleasing aroma of Ma's homemade vegetable stew. It was one of Tom's favorites. And one of Ma's. It made the food go farther.

But Ma and Pa had a farm they could live off. And no one could complain about that.

The garden was a quiet place. A pleasant place for one to think and just be. But it proved to be a lot of work, too.

Lauren Crawford stretched her aching muscles. The tension was real. And the sting was real. How could it be that her body still protested the simple daily tasks she undertook?

Grabbing for her basket, now nearly full of vegetables, she stood and moved toward the row of tomatoes. It didn't matter that her father despised her little garden. She loved it. Every-thing about it—working with her hands, producing life from the soil, tending to the seedlings, all of it.

Kneeling, she spread out her skirt. This was one of her plainer dresses. Mother would not be happy she had been in the dirt, but Mother was never happy with her or anything she did.

Lauren grasped the tomato closest to her—plump, full, and a brilliant shade of red. But it wouldn't break away from the vine. Twisting it, she pulled more firmly. Still, it persisted. She tugged all the more. At last, the tomato gave way, throwing her off balance and exploding on the bodice of her dress.

Her elbows stung from her collision with the ground as she was showered with bright red pulp.

Mother would be livid.

"You might should use a knife," a voice said from behind her.

She jerked her head around.

The young man from the previous week's encounter stood tall and proud, a crooked smile on his face. He was almost handsome.

A tingle shot through Lauren. Excitement? Concern? What was he doing here?

Righting herself, she brushed off the worst of the tomato juice. Her dress would be stained for certain.

Shifting to stand, she leaned forward to push herself up but noticed an outstretched hand.

The young man now stood over her.

She hesitated a moment then slid a hand into his. Before she had taken another breath, she was on her feet. "Thank you, sir."

The corners of his mouth lifted.

She offered him a kind smile. Then she remembered where

she was. And who she was. Her brows furrowed. Was he stalking her? "What are you doing here?"

His smile fell. "My apologies. I have business with your father. That is, I presume he's your father—the plantation owner."

She nodded.

"I have just rented one of the fields."

A tenant farmer. So that's why he was on her father's land last week.

His brows gathered. "You didn't think I was following you, did you?"

Lauren's face warmed. "No, of course not."

"That's the kind of empty-headed, self-absorbed thing I would expect from a woman of your..." He let his sentence fade. Did he think better of his words?

"A woman of my what?" she challenged.

"It's not important." He stepped away. "I will be on my way to—"

"Wait!" She reached out, touching his shoulder before she could stop herself.

He halted.

"I want to know what you were going to say. A woman of my what?"

Turning, he put his hands on his belt, looked off into the distance, and sighed. Then he met her eyes. "A woman of your society."

Her mouth opened. She closed it again. What could she say to such a statement?

"I mean no disrespect." He held out his hands. "I only mean to say that southern belles have a...certain way about them."

She flared her nostrils. "And that's all I am? A southern belle?"

Silence fell between them. And he shrugged. "It's not meant as a slur, miss."

"No?" She quirked a brow and planted a hand on her hip.

What could she say? He seemed determined on his opinion. There were many things she wanted to say, but no words would form.

"I think I should go."

"No, please, allow me." She picked up her basket of vegetables and stomped off toward the nearby house.

How dare he suggest that she would be shallow, and thoughtless, and simply...simply...

Either way, she would *not* let him know it bothered her. Several steps away, she paused and turned. "Good day to you, Mr..." Lauren realized she didn't know his name.

"Matthews. The name is Tom Matthews."

"Very well. Good day, Mr. Matthews." With that, she spun and did not look back.

Chapter Two

"See the dog run."

"Good," Lauren cheered. Isaac had finally read his first sentence, and she couldn't be happier. All of their hard work was proving worthwhile. "Now, you try it, Millie."

"See the dog run." The little girl beamed at Lauren. She hadn't so much as glanced at the book.

Lauren gave her a sweet smile. "Let's try the next sentence." She pointed to the words below the sentence Isaac had read.

Millie stared at the page, moved the book closer to her face, but could not produce anything.

Scooting closer, Lauren leaned over. "Let's sound it out together."

Millie nodded.

"Th—" Lauren started.

The small girl pushed her tongue against her teeth to replicate the sound.

"The ka-ka-ka—"

Millie continued following Lauren's lead.

"...cat r-r-r-r-a-a-a—"

The door to the tiny house flung open. Millie and Isaac's mother was on her feet in a moment. Was she preparing to protect her children? What manner of instinct was that? Lauren could not tear her eyes away.

In moments, the small space was invaded by two men carrying the children's father. One man was black, another sharecropper perhaps. The other was none other than Mr. Tom Matthews.

Lauren had nowhere to hide. How to escape discovery? She was trapped.

Mrs. Amos cleared the dining table and the two men set Mr. Amos on it.

Only then did Lauren take notice of his leg. It bled horribly. She pulled the children to herself, pressing their faces into her skirt as she turned her head.

What had happened to him?

Mrs. Amos took charge immediately. "A blade?" She leaned over her husband's leg, already a cloth in her hand.

"His axe got away from him," Tom said. "I think it's bad."

Mrs. Amos nodded.

Tom and the other man took a step back. Only then did Tom look in her direction. His eyes caught and held hers.

Did he wonder what she was doing here? Could he put the pieces together? Of course, he would. But would he tell her father?

His jaw set and the line of his mouth thinned. He did not look pleased.

She dropped her head. How could she continue to face him?

"Miz Crawford, could you take the children outside?" Mrs. Amos' eyes were on her.

She nodded. Keeping her hands on the shoulders of the children, she maneuvered them around the opposite side of the table from Tom and out the door.

Once they were outside and in the open, she breathed deeply.

Millie and Isaac still clung to her skirt but soon loosened their hold.

"May we play?" Isaac looked up at her.

Lauren looked into his pleading eyes. What did she expect? They didn't understand. Or maybe they did and wished to distract themselves. Either way, it was a good idea. So, she nodded.

They took off.

A slab of wood nearby seemed as if it could serve as a makeshift bench. She all but collapsed on it. What was she going to do?

Her father's angry face flashed before her mind's eye. He would not like what she had been up to these past couple of weeks—the fact that she had been spending time with this family would be bad enough. But teaching the children? It would surely enrage him.

The door creaked.

Lauren jerked around to see Tom emerge. She turned away, but that didn't stop him from stepping toward her. His presence hanging over her.

"Are you all right?" His voice was so caring, so tender.

She shifted to peer at him once more. When she caught his eyes, they were as sympathetic as his voice had been.

"I am." She let out a deep breath. "A bit shaken, but I am well."

He nodded, watching the children as they ran about in the field. "I hope he keeps the leg."

Lauren nodded. What would happen to the little family if Mr. Amos lost his leg and wasn't able to farm?

What if he had bled out in the field? How fortunate that Tom and the other sharecropper had helped him.

"Thank you." Lauren's voice was weak. Even she heard that it was so.

His eyes were on her. "For what?"

"For helping him. And bringing him home."

Tom nodded. "I'm just glad I was there." His eyes drifted to the ground.

Lauren hated that her thoughts turned to her own problems. Would Tom speak with her father? What did Tom think of her teaching the children? Probably what any white man would—that it was ridiculous, even vile.

Closing her eyes, the need to ask became overwhelming. She had to know. How best to broach it? "Please, don't tell my father."

His eyes were on her then, boring into her. Dare she meet them?

After several moments of silence, she did.

His amber eyes were deep. They warmed her and put her on edge at the same time. Her stomach fluttered.

He opened his mouth.

The door hinges squealed as the sharecropper stepped out.

Tom shifted his focus to the man. "Is it bad?"

The man nodded. "Mrs. Amos cleaned it and stitched him up. We can only hope for the best now."

"He needs medicine," Lauren interjected.

Tom and the sharecropper stared at her. What was that in Tom's eyes before he looked away?

Heat suffused her being as realization overcame her. Of course, Mr. Amos couldn't afford a doctor. How could she be so thoughtless? None of these men could afford that kind of care.

But her father could.

"Perhaps I could tell my father—"

Tom held up a hand. "Mrs. Amos has done what she can. We have to wait."

Was Tom worried about her? About her father finding out about her close association with the sharecropper family? Did he care so?

Yes, her father could be a hard man. But surely he would see what was right—that Mr. Amos needed help.

Still, as she watched Tom, she decided to trust his judgment.

The field stretched long in front of Tom. What must it be like to own so much land? To be the master of such a domain? One day, he promised himself, one day.

He continued to put distance between himself and the Amoses' small parcel of land. It was only right he should stop in on Elijah Amos, but nothing good had come from it.

The man was not doing well—delirious with fever. Sure sign of infection. A sad tale for certain.

This made him think on Lauren. Should he go to her father? Would the man have mercy and provide the care Lauren was sure he would? Would the older man then discover that Tom knew about her teaching the Amos children and had not spoken out? That would not bode well.

Yet, he could not bring himself to tell the man, to call down her father's ire. He did not wish for her to be the brunt of anyone's anger. Least of all someone who could hurt her.

Tom had not had many interactions with the older man, but the plantation master's reputation was well known. It was said he had held his slaves in place with an iron fist and ready whip. Would he rein his daughter in the same way?

When Tom had gone to the man to set up his tenancy, the older man had been...difficult. Something lay just beneath the surface. Something hard.

Even so, Lauren was not like other women of her class.

That myth had been dispelled the moment he walked into the shack of a house the Amos family called home. But the illusion had been crumbling even before that moment.

He should have suspected. Had he not seen her cross his field from the direction of the Amos land every day carrying the same load of books and slates as the first day they met? How had he not put it together?

Her kindness and selflessness in her interactions with him had been enough to crack his hard-edged assumptions about her. Now, they had been shattered altogether.

He crossed the stream between his field and Elijah's—the last barrier. Now he only needed to walk up the hill and to his crops.

As he neared his cornfield, however, the scent of light perfume reached his nostrils. He looked up. Lauren Crawford was there, amongst the stalks, arms crossed in front of her chest as she paced.

He took several long strides, closing the remaining distance. Stopping just short of where she stood, he was surprised when she did not seem to notice. So, he announced his presence. "I didn't expect to see you here."

She jumped but maintained her balance. When she laid eyes on him, she frowned, and her brow furrowed.

He responded primarily from the guilty feelings rising in him. "I didn't mean to upset you. Did you need something?"

"I am worried about Mr. Amos. Have you heard anything?"

Could he not avoid this? He didn't want her to know. But if she must, why did he need to be the bearer of the news?

"I just came from there." Wanting to look away, but finding it impossible, he stood transfixed by her hazel gaze.

Lauren stepped toward him, eyes wide. "And?"

She appeared so hopeful. Tom wished he had better news. "It's not good."

Her face fell.

He longed to reach out and comfort her in some way, but he thought it best he keep his hands to himself. "There is fever. And probably infection."

Lauren covered her face with a hand.

Her distress became more than he could bear. He stepped forward, closer to her side.

She lowered her hand.

Tom halted.

"He needs a doctor," her statement was simple, as if it were the most logical thing to say.

Tom grimaced. She spoke the impossible. If only all had such luxury.

"And I'm going to make sure he gets one." She spun, skirts flaring, and walked in the direction of the mansion.

Tom reached out and grabbed for her arm.

She stopped, turning her head toward him.

"Don't." He was surprised by the fervor of his own voice. "If your father finds out you've been..." He let his sentence trail.

Lauren shifted her body to angle in his direction. "But I have to. I have to risk it. I can't do nothing and wonder. I'd regret it for the rest of my life."

"But I don't want..." He had almost said too much.

"What?"

He searched her eyes.

"You don't want what?"

Tom sighed. "I don't want to see you hurt."

A smile tugged at the corners of her mouth. "He's my father. He will help me."

Though he was doubtful, Tom nodded. Something in him ached to hold her, but he resisted.

She offered him a small smile. "But I thank you, sir. You are a true gentleman."

He laughed at that. No one had ever called him that before.

An awkward silence fell between them.

Lauren spoke. "I'd best go. Mr. Amos needs that doctor."

Tom nodded. "Be careful."

"I always am." She gave him a grin. Then moved off in the opposite direction once more.

The great door in the downstairs entry slammed. Father must be home.

Lauren stepped from her room and padded silently down the hallway toward the stairs.

Pa's voice thundered throughout the open space of the entryway, bouncing off the high ceilings and ringing in Lauren's ears.

She closed her eyes. *Why, God? Why today of all days?*

But it was like this most days. At least more often than not. Why was Pa so often in these moods? The war had changed him. Or did she only lie to herself? Had he always been this way? Had the war simply removed the slaves that buffered his anger?

Shrinking back, she inched toward the safety of her room. This was not the time.

But did Mr. Amos have time for her hesitancy? For her to be fearful of her own father? She halted her retreat, looking at the floor. No, he did not.

Glancing in the direction of the stairs, she caught bits and pieces of her father's angry words. Perhaps she could calm his ire. He was her father, after all. And he wasn't upset with her.

What had angered him today? She could not be sure. It was always something—money, crops, the lack of help.

Perhaps the lack of control. But most certainly not her. No, she was his little daffodil.

Swallowing hard, she pushed down her trepidations and moved cautiously toward the grand staircase.

Her father's voice began to fade. Did he move into another area of the house?

She descended the stairs. One of the hired hands, Abraham, stood in the foyer, head hung. So this was who intercepted her father's wrath today. Tomorrow, who knew?

Her skirts rustled against the banister.

Abraham looked up. A smile graced his lips. He had always had a warm spot for Lauren. His daughter and Lauren had grown up together. They had been the best of friends despite Pa's insistence that the two girls not spend so much time with each other. But it could not be helped. Not when Abraham's wife was Lauren's nursemaid while Lauren's own mother was otherwise occupied.

All of Lauren's earliest memories were of her mammy. She had a difficult time recalling her own mother's face during those years. Except when Lauren had made the mistake of picking those flowers for Ma. That she remembered quite clearly.

"What can I do for ya, Miz Lauren?" Abraham's deep voice broke into Lauren's sad reverie.

She met his eyes. "Nothing, thank you. I need to speak with my father."

Abraham's eyes widened. "Your Pa's in a mighty foul mood." The man glanced in the direction of the family parlor. "Maybe you should come back—"

Lauren put a hand on his arm. "It can't wait."

Saddened eyes turned toward the floor, but he held a hand in the direction of the parlor.

Lauren did what she could to gather her courage as she

moved past him. Why did she need to? This was her *father*. He *loved* her. Right?

As she neared the parlor, her father's voice still sounded through the space, though it had quieted somewhat. Who was he speaking with?

The door to the parlor was ajar. And though her father's voice no longer pressed with volume, it maintained an edge. But the words were somewhat muffled by the door. If she wanted to, she could lean closer to the slight opening and listen. Dare she?

There was a pause.

Should she make her presence known now? She drew in a ragged breath. Her heart beat wildly.

Closing her eyes, she raised a hand and tapped the door three times.

Silence.

She knocked again. "Pa?" Her voice wavered.

"Come." Pa's voice was firm.

Lauren pushed the door open and stepped into the family parlor. Her father stood at the large window across the room. The light coming in from behind him silhouetted his figure, making it difficult for her to discern the nuances of his face. But she saw the scowl on her mother's face quite well.

Ma sat on a settee near Pa, but she had angled her body in the direction of the door.

Lauren wished she could melt into the floor. She had prepared herself to face Pa, but speaking in front of Ma was another thing entirely.

An awkward silence fell over the room.

Her parents continued to stare at her.

Pa cocked his head. "Did you need something?"

Why couldn't she read at least something in his features? That might give her a cue for her next decision.

She nodded, shot a glance at Ma, and then latched her gaze

to Pa. That was best. Perhaps that way she could make it through.

"I have...been told...that is, I heard...what I mean to say is...there is a sharecropper on the plantation that has been injured. And now he is very sick with fever."

Pa didn't move.

Ma shifted only slightly, raising an eyebrow and looking toward Pa.

Lauren's hands began to burn. She looked down. Had she been wringing them so tightly? Forcing her fingers to intertwine, she set them at hip level.

"And what do you think I should do about this?" Pa's voice was calm. A good sign.

Lauren tried to keep her excitement down. There was hope. "He needs a doctor. And medicine." She sighed. "But he does not have money for either."

Pa nodded.

Sensing Ma's eyes boring into her, Lauren felt sweat trickling between her shoulder blades. But she refused to look in her mother's direction again.

"And just how did you come by this knowledge? This... awareness of Mr. Amos' injury?"

"I..." Should she tell the truth? Or maintain her story? It was wrong to lie. Even for the good of another.

But was this for Mr. Amos' good? Or for her own? Wait...

Had she told Pa it was Mr. Amos?

She sought her father's face.

He stepped forward, into the room's light. His brows were furrowed and his mouth a thin line.

What did he know? "I was—"

Pa held up a hand. "Don't bother. I know."

Lauren stepped back from the intensity of his gaze and swallowed against the lump forming in her throat.

"And I don't think I need to tell you how disappointed I am in you." His voice remained calm but took on a tense edge.

Tears pricked at the back of her eyes and her throat tightened. "Pa, I just—"

He waved a hand across the space between them. "I don't want your reasons, your excuses. Somewhere along the way, you have become deceived about the way things are. No more. It's time for you to be...enlightened."

"What...what are you saying?" Moisture filled Lauren's eyes. Everything lost focus in the blur of her tears.

"You are not to teach these or any other black children, is that understood?"

Lauren couldn't form words. It was as if the breath had been torn from her body.

"It's not kind, can't you see that, Lauren? What are you teaching them for? The world won't accept them as anything but workers."

She shook her head. What was *he* saying? Lauren put a hand to her mouth to stem the tide.

Pa had advanced until he stood in front of her. Raising his hands, he closed his fingers around her upper arms then— gentle, but holding her still.

"If you insist on continuing, if I find out you are still teaching those children, I will have them evicted from this plantation. And you can know they will not find work anywhere in this or any surrounding state as long as I can help it."

Lauren blinked several times before she could meet her father's gaze again. His blue eyes were cold and hard. He meant what he said.

She nodded. "Yes, Pa." The words didn't seem to come from her but from outside of herself somehow.

He pulled her to his chest. "How can I make you understand? I am doing this for your own good, Daffodil."

Lauren wanted to pull away, to run. But where could she go?

Tom Matthews moved with measured steps. He had a destination and a purpose.

Days had passed. Many days. Still, Lauren Crawford did not show her face anywhere near the Amos property. Or his.

Perhaps she was not able to convince her father to pay for a doctor. That was one thing. But why would she desert them altogether?

It wasn't like her. Or what he thought he knew of her.

Had something happened between her and her father? The man hadn't hurt her, had he?

Tom's heart constricted. He shouldn't have let her go up against the man. But she had convinced him that her father would not raise a hand to his own child. Then again, the man had been a slave master. Perhaps beatings had become second nature to him.

As he approached the manor house, he detoured toward the far side. Would he find her in her garden? If not, his chances of seeing her would likely vanish.

Nearing the small segment of the property set aside for Lauren, his heart fell. She was not there.

He stopped. Glancing around, he hoped against hope he might catch sight of her somewhere.

Nothing.

After some moments, he turned back toward his property, letting out a long breath. What was he going to do? Should he confront her father? Insist that he be allowed to see her? Would that make her father suspicious? It may mean the end of Tom's tenancy. Was it worth the risk?

He stopped.

Dare he? But he barely knew her. Still, he could no longer rest if he didn't settle this in his mind.

Making his way around the large house, he walked to the massive door. He paused for a long moment. Was he sure? He pictured Lauren in his mind's eye. Yes, she was worth it.

Raising a fist to the door, he paused. Why was this so important? Was she so important? He'd have to figure out the answer later. Because for now, seeing her well and whole mattered.

He knocked on the door.

Several moments passed before it opened and a thin, tall black man stood before him. His hair was graying and the crinkles at the corners of his eyes betrayed his years.

"What can I do for you?" the man asked.

Tom stood to his full height. "I need to speak with—"

"Tom?" a voice behind the black man echoed in the cavernous space.

He craned his neck, attempting to look around the man's slender frame.

Lauren stood on the grand staircase, a few steps from the bottom.

Tom's gaze took her in from top to bottom. She did not appear to be in any sort of distress. There were no visible marks upon her.

"Do you know this man, Miz Lauren?"

"This is one of the tenant farmers." She glided down the remaining steps and across the tiled floor. "I asked him to come by and help me with my tomato plants."

Lauren and the tall black man exchanged a long look. There was more communicated than Tom understood. Certainly more than what was said.

At length, the butler stepped back and let Lauren step around him.

"We will be out in my garden. Can you send for Mammy and have her bring my hat?"

"Yes, Miz Lauren." The man moved farther into the house, disappearing down a hall.

"Thank you so much for coming, Mr. Matthews. I had forgotten our meeting." Lauren beamed at him.

He furrowed his brow and lowered his voice. "I came to make sure you were all right."

She shook her head. "I have been so concerned about those tomato plants. Are you certain they can be saved?"

Tom crooked a brow in her direction. "We'll just have to look at them. I won't know until I see."

The butler came from the same hallway he had disappeared down, only this time, he escorted a black woman. She was shorter, but just as slender, as the butler. And she kept looking in the air as if a flying insect hovered about.

As the pair neared Lauren, she reached for the older woman's arm.

"Thank you for bringing my hat, Mammy."

Tom did not see anything in the older woman's hands. He thought to say something but decided it would be best if he remained quiet.

Keeping an arm around Mammy's, Lauren shifted her focus to Tom. "Mammy will chaperone. Shall we?"

Chaperone? The woman seemed barely aware of where she was. Had something happened to the older woman? Either way, he read from Lauren's nod that they should go. Stepping back, he held out an arm indicating for the women to step out of the grand entrance. Then he led them to the small garden at the back of the oversized structure.

Lauren settled Mammy on a wrought iron bench nearby, adjusting her skirts and fussing over her as if the chaperone were the child. Only then did Lauren turn to Tom, moving to where he stood amidst her plants.

Now next to him, she offered an uneasy smile and knelt before the tomatoes.

Tom crouched beside her, fighting his confusion. He was not here to solve all these mysteries, but to ensure Lauren was well.

He scrutinized her features, watching as the light played against the angles of her face when she leaned forward, tending to the vines. Even her hair shone a brilliant chestnut in the rays of the sun.

If only he could lean in and take in her perfume again. From this distance he inhaled but a hint of the fragrance. Honeysuckle?

She lifted her face and met his gaze.

He looked away, his face warming.

"Why have you come?" Her voice was soft. Almost a whisper.

"I worried." He faced her again. Her hazel eyes warmed him all the more.

"Worried? About me?"

"Because of your father." Tom lowered his voice, glancing around. "I feared what your father might have done to you."

She jerked back, pulling away from him. "My father would *never* hurt me."

Tom followed her retreat with his eyes. Something didn't seem right about her reaction. And yet, she was unharmed. Had he overstepped?

"Then what happened?"

Lauren moved to the next plant. "I don't know what you mean."

"You said you would talk with him about Mr. Amos."

She shrugged.

Shrugged.

Was that all?

"Do you no longer care?"

She paused for a moment. Then started her work again, pruning the vines. Moving to another plant, she angled her body so her back was to him.

"In case you were wondering, Mr. Amos still lives. Though he continues to fight the sickness."

Nothing.

"He may yet die."

Silence. Or did she just sniffle?

"And it no longer matters to you?"

She shook her head.

A fire burned in him. How could he have been so blind? "I was wrong about you. I thought you were different. But you're not."

"Maybe I'm not." Why did her voice sound so apathetic? Had she numbed to the situation?

"How could you abandon that family...those children... when they need you most?"

She shifted so she could bring her knees to her chest. "You don't know anything."

"Then school me," he spat out as he stood.

Lauren buried her face in her knees and her shoulders shook.

Tom was prepared to spin on the balls of his feet and walk away, but the shaking of her body gave him pause.

Nothing was as it seemed. Her care for Mammy, the long look exchanged with the butler... There was more going on here.

He blew out a long breath and crouched behind her. "Please. Tell me what's happened."

She remained silent for several moments. Until he was convinced she would not speak at all.

Then her voice, quiet as it was, broke into the silence. "I...I don't know what to do anymore."

It became impossible for him not to reach out to her, so he laid a hand on her shoulder.

She leaned into his chest. "I have nowhere to go. No one to trust."

"You can trust me," he whispered into her hair. And he had never meant anything more in his entire life.

Chapter Three

Tom slowed his father's horse as he approached the small town. Did he have enough? It would have to be.

Maneuvering the steed down the main stretch, he found his way to the clinic. Pulling the reins, he brought the horse to a halt. He then jumped down and secured the animal to a post.

He swallowed hard as he looked up at the sign. What would come of this? Tom took in a breath and pushed the door open.

The town doctor sat at his desk reading through a book that had a drawing of an eye on it. It made Tom's stomach turn a little.

"Dr. Archer." Tom approached, trying to calm his racing heart.

"Yes, sir, what can I do for you?" The doctor continued to make notes in his journal.

"I'm a tenant farmer on the Crawford plantation. One of the sharecroppers on the property, Mr. Amos, was badly injured by an axe. His wife cleaned and stitched him, but he's had fever ever since. It's bad. They don't have much money. But I have some."

Tom reached into his pocket, pulling out everything he had earned and saved for his move out west. He laid it on the desk. "Will that be enough?"

The doctor looked at the money and then at Tom. He seemed to be studying Tom. Did he wonder if he should help a sharecropper? Did he suspect that Mr. Amos was black? Would Tom wonder the same thing if he were in this man's shoes?

To Tom, Elijah Amos was another farmer. He didn't have the luxury of placing people in different categories. But he knew that some people did.

After some moments, the doctor drew in a long breath. "Take me to the man."

Tom nodded and watched as the doctor stood and went for his medical bag, filling it with an odd assortment of things.

Then Dr. Archer stepped toward Tom. "Let's go."

Tom looked at the money on the desk. Wasn't the doctor going to secure it?

"Keep your money until I do my work. Same as anyone else."

Tom nodded, grabbing the money, and pocketing it. He led the doctor outside. They each mounted their steeds and pushed off toward the Crawford property on the edge of Waverly.

Time passed quickly as they rode, yet it seemed to take hours to reach the shack that the Amos family called home.

Tom glanced over to gauge the doctor's reaction as they dismounted.

Dr. Archer didn't so much as flinch.

"This way." Tom waved the doctor in as he moved to the door. He knocked lightly.

Isaac answered the door. He stared up at the two intruders.

Tom offered him a smile. "I've brought the doctor to see your Pa."

Still not speaking, Isaac moved out of the way and let the men pass.

Moving farther into the small house, Tom urged the doctor ahead, toward the designated bedroom area. It had simply been screened off.

Mrs. Amos sat on the mattress next to her husband's still form. She held his hand to her chest and wept.

The doctor rushed forward. Any hint that he'd had any qualms about skin color was forgotten. His hands moved over Mr. Amos' head, lifted his eyelids, and looked into his eyes. Then he grabbed Elijah's wrist.

Mrs. Amos did not move, save a gentle rocking motion. She did not give any indication she was even aware of the doctor's presence. But she continued humming an old hymn.

The doctor hung his head.

Tom stepped forward. "What?"

"Keep your money, son. There's nothing I can do here." Dr. Archer stepped toward the door, pausing next to Tom, and placing a hand on his shoulder. "There was probably nothing I could have done no matter when you came for me. His leg wound is severe."

Numb, Tom nodded. Was the doctor speaking truthfully? Or just being kind? Had Elijah Amos been doomed from the moment the axe connected with his leg?

What would become of this small family?

Lauren took her seat at the family dinner table. Things had been relatively calm in the house for the last week. She'd made a concerted effort not to stir trouble. And Pa seemed to believe she had become compliant. Perhaps she had.

Stealing a glance at the head of the table, she studied Pa. He had engaged their guest, a visiting plantation master, in talk of the latest government regulations.

Pa continued to converse as if he did not sense her gaze on him. Indeed, maybe he did not.

But she felt eyes boring into her. Shifting her focus to the left, her gaze collided with Ma's. Was it even possible to please that woman?

Lauren lowered her focus to her plate and prayed Ma would become distracted. Moments later, the hairs on the back of her neck no longer prickled and she relaxed.

Only then could she give any attention to her dinner. Paying heed to the dishing out of food was all she could muster. But eating was beyond her with thoughts so entangled with Tom.

She had not seen him since that afternoon earlier in the week when he had comforted her. While she had sought solace for the moment, his words offered more. Could she trust in them? In him? Could a tenant farmer be her salvation?

"Seems I'll have another parcel of land to let out soon enough." Pa's voice boomed. Louder than it needed to.

Lauren glanced across the table.

His gaze was on her.

"Is that so?" His guest scooped potatoes into his mouth.

Had something happened with Tom? Had Pa discovered their budding relationship and decided to get rid of Tom? Is that what was going on between her and Tom?

"Yes," Pa continued, letting his eyes rest on Lauren's face. "Seems one of my sharecroppers died yesterday."

Lauren's breath caught. Died? Her heart sank. Mr. Amos had died? What would become of Mrs. Amos? Isaac and Millie? They would become lost in the world. With no way to live, to sustain themselves? The warmth drained from her face.

"It is no matter." Pa sighed and looked down at his plate.

"Good riddance is what I say," the other plantation master said.

Lauren's stomach turned.

"Indeed. I choose not to suffer these sad cases. I had a runaway slave situation a while back. Had to handle it decisively. Couldn't let the other slaves thinking they could just up and leave." Though Pa still spoke with his friend, his gaze rested on Lauren.

"That's what must be done." The man's eyes moved between Pa and Lauren, brows furrowed. Did he wonder at the curious state of Pa's glare?

But Lauren barely noticed the man. Did Pa have a tale of a runaway slave she did not know? How could he? Unless...

Lauren's mind peeled back the years until she found herself standing in a field with Mammy's daughter Grace, Lauren's best friend in the whole world. Grace had never asked Lauren for anything until that one night not so long ago. And Lauren could not refuse her. Grace wanted to escape into the darkness, having arranged to join the Underground Railroad.

Though Lauren was loathed to part with her friend, she could not deny Grace the opportunity to be free. While they had been girls together, Grace had been sheltered by their friendship. But as they grew, things changed. Everyone started treating Grace differently. It became more difficult for her.

And then Grace fell in love. It was young love. Too young. But she and her beau wanted to be married. Only, Pa sold Grace's love off before the two could do so.

Still, Grace refused to be separated from him.

Lauren shivered at the memory. That night, Grace would meet her beloved on the Underground Railroad. All Lauren had to do was help Grace get to her beau's plantation. How could she not?

Pa's voice pulled her from the memory.

"It was a young slave girl," he began, his words directed to his guest, but very much for her. "Found her at a nearby plantation. Tried to run away with another slave I had sold off. Thought they could be free and get married. How ridiculous."

The cruelty in his tone tore at Lauren's heart.

"What happened?" Lauren could not stop the question that pressed out of her lips.

All eyes were on her.

Including Pa's.

"They were shot," Pa said as if he delivered the latest crop yield estimates. Then he took a swig from his glass.

Her stomach convulsed. Lauren pushed back from the table, one hand on her mouth, one on her stomach, and ran. She didn't stop until she was next to the stream between Mr. Amos' and Tom's fields.

Falling to her knees, she lost her composure and her stomach by the side of the creek. She shook from the physical upheaval as well as from the turmoil within.

Grace. Her sweet Grace. Lauren never knew—never knew of her fate.

Mammy—Grace's mother—and Abraham, her father. How they must have suffered.

A cry worked its way up and out of Lauren's mouth. She groaned, doubling over. All of these years, she had known something happened to Mammy. That much was clear. How had she never guessed? Never understood the sadness that plagued Abraham? They must have known all along.

She clung to the ground beneath her hands, digging her nails into the damp grass. The ache was unbearable. Oh to be comforted right now by Mammy's sweet voice, Abraham's tender gaze, or Tom's embrace...

Tom's embrace?

She sat straighter. Did she truly want for that?

Yes, so very much.

Hadn't he told her she could trust him?

But how would she find him? She had no idea where he lived. Sinking back down, she bemoaned her situation. Could she face her father again? But without Tom, where else could she go?

To the Amos home.

Tom laid his mother's prized cornbread on the table as well as a sack of vegetables. It wasn't much, but it was all his family could spare.

Mrs. Amos nodded.

And he understood. She was grateful but knew not how to say so. Her eyes told a story of a world upturned, a future—uncertain. Her situation screamed of injustice, but what was there to do? What could he, a tenant farmer, offer in terms of aid? The Amos family was not friendless, but there wasn't much their friends could do for them.

Tom wished there were. But his hands were tied. So, he bobbed his head once more and turned toward the door and found relief in the fresh air once outside.

He leaned against the side of the house. How could God allow such things to happen? But Tom saw it everywhere. People hurting, dying, suffering. It was no way to live.

His breath caught.

And his next breath was short.

A weight slammed into his chest.

Would he be able to draw in another breath?

Stop it!

Sucking in a long breath, he pushed it out slowly. Then,

forcing the next one in just as calmly, he measured its release as well. Over and over, he did so until his breaths came easily.

His head felt lighter, but his breathing was steady.

Gazing at the horizon, he spotted a figure in the distance. A woman, dressed in fine clothes with long dark hair pulled up off her shoulders. Could it be Lauren?

Certain it was a daydream, perhaps a symptom of his daze; he shook his head and blinked several times.

She continued to move along the tree line. Perhaps it *was* Lauren.

Should he move to intercept her? Or leave her be? Had she come to pay her respects to Mrs. Amos?

Before he could decide, he found himself walking toward her. His gaze trained on her, he noted the minute she became aware of his presence.

She halted. Her arms wrapped around her stomach.

Was something amiss?

Then her hands covered her face.

His pace quickened until he stood an arm's length away. Hands itching to touch her, he fought that urge. It would do no good to frighten her, but his gaze went where his fingers longed. He drank in the sight of her.

"Lauren," he breathed. Dare he step closer?

She closed the distance between them, laying her forehead on his chest. "I hardly know where to begin."

His hands cupped her upper arms. "I'm not going anywhere. I'll listen when you're ready."

Laying her hands on his chest, she looked up into his eyes. If he had not already fallen under her spell, he would have in that moment. Her eyes were deeper than any pit he had known. And as much as something within her called to him, seeking, there was also an offer, a hope, a promise.

What was happening?

"My father. You were right about him."

"Has he hurt you?" Tom searched her anew for injuries.

"Not like that." Tears brimmed anew. "But in the ways that matter. Here." She pressed a hand to her heart.

He ducked his head, biting at his lip, so she wouldn't see his anger.

Lauren laid a hand to the side of his face.

Tom raised his head to meet her eyes again.

"He had my best friend killed."

Opening his mouth, Tom then found himself unable to speak.

Lauren sniffled. "Years ago. She was a slave. Killed when she tried to run away. But he never told me. Until today. And he took great pleasure in doing so this evening." She looked toward the horizon.

Tom still couldn't find words. Hadn't he fought for her father to retain that very right? Otis died for plantation masters to continue to treat people that way. Otis...

"Tom? Are you okay?"

Lauren's face loomed in front of his. Her eyes wide and trusting. How could he tell her? "I'm sorry. It's nothing."

"You're certain?" Her brows furrowed.

He nodded.

She looked to the ground.

Had he said something wrong?

Her eyes flickered to his. "I know that every man of age had to fight in the war to protect the slavery laws."

Tom gazed at her for a few moments. How had she guessed? There was a depth, and such sadness in her eyes in that moment.

An unspoken question hung between them. The questions that every man in the war had to face. Questions about slavery.

She let out a breath and stared at his chest. "Do you think runaway slaves deserved to be shot?"

Tom pulled her closer. "How can you ask me that? Of course not."

Lauren wouldn't meet his eyes.

"I was young, forced into the Confederate Army. Just trying to do my best to stay alive. Especially after..." His hold on her slackened. He had almost said too much.

"After what?" She looked at him.

Tom pushed a hand through his hair and licked his lips. "I joined the Confederate Army for two reasons: they were going to draft us anyway, and because my cousin Otis and I signed on together."

Looking for Lauren to say something yielded nothing. She kept her eyes on his, waiting for him to continue. Neither pushing nor prodding, just giving him the space to share as he wished, as much as he wished. And he was grateful for the room to do so.

But he wanted to continue. Tom had not talked about Otis in so long. And even then, he'd never truly shared what happened. He just couldn't.

"Otis was never serious. Always horsing around. Even when it came to the war. But when it was time for battle...and we were in a tough spot, he..."

Lauren rubbed a hand up and down his arm.

"A small contingency of Union soldiers found their way into our bunker. I don't know how. We fought them off. But one of them wouldn't go down. I remember his bayonet, ready to run me through. And Otis...he...he jumped between the soldier and me. The man stabbed it right into his heart."

Closing her eyes, a tear escaped down Lauren's face.

"He was dead before he hit the ground. As was the Union soldier."

Tom drew in a ragged breath.

"But I will never forget Otis's face as long as I live."

Lauren hooked a hand behind Tom's neck and drew him into her embrace.

It was sweet, to hold her fully to himself. He could believe, in that moment, that anything was possible between them. That she wasn't a plantation master's daughter, or that he wasn't a simple farmer's son. But that they were simply Tom and Lauren. And that love was all that mattered.

Because, bless it all, he loved her.

A gentle breeze blew over them. It was cool. But it did not chill Lauren. Her body was warmed by the safety of the cocoon created by Tom's arms.

She opened her eyes. The sky had exploded in a myriad of pinks, oranges, and purples. Had they lingered so long?

Reluctantly, she pulled away.

His eyes were on hers.

"If I don't return to the house, Mammy will worry."

Tom nodded. "And your parents."

Lauren looked off to the horizon. "I don't know." She met his eyes again. "Pa would worry, except…" Sighing, she turned her face toward the ground. "I'm not sure of anything with him anymore."

"And your mother?" Tom's brows creased.

Her eyes were on his again, perhaps a bit sharp. He flinched under her gaze. "My mother has never concerned herself with my whereabouts or my well-being. Only my behavior."

"That can't be true."

Lauren studied Tom's disbelieving features. Was he so innocent? Did his mother not treat him thusly? Perhaps his mother was more like Mammy. "I have few early memories of my mother. Only Mammy. And Grace. My mother kept her distance. I never understood why. I thought…" Emotion welling, she looked down again. "I thought maybe it was me. Maybe I wasn't good enough."

Tom's eyes softened and he opened his mouth.

But Lauren didn't give him a chance to speak. "So, I tried my best to please her. Mammy once told me that Ma's favorite flowers were lilies. We had a section in the garden full of lilies. And one day I…picked some for her."

Tom remained quiet, listening, holding her hands, and rubbing the backs of her fingers with his thumbs.

"Was she ever angry." Hot tears stung Lauren's eyes. *Still? After all this time?* "I learned that day what a beating felt like."

Tom reached for her, but she pressed a hand to his chest, halting him. She had to finish.

"Mammy told me something that day that I didn't understand until much later." Lauren's gaze drifted off toward some point in the distance. "I had an older sister. She died from a strange fever. Ma loved her so very much. Lily. It broke Ma's heart. Apparently, she just didn't have it in her to risk loving another child. Those flowers had been planted on Lily's first birthday."

She didn't bother with the tears flowing down her face as she ended the tale. When she peered into Tom's eyes expecting pity, she found sadness, yes, but something more…something deeper. Something she had only found in Mammy's eyes.

Compassion.

So, she let him enfold her once again in his embrace. And let herself hope that perhaps in this man she might find the ability for her heart to heal. *God, may it be so.*

Chapter Four

Tom approached the manor house. He could not remember ever being more nervous. Pausing at the door, he rubbed his sweating palms on his trouser legs.

Looking to the heavens, he lifted a prayer for strength and wisdom. But was this not the craziest thing he had ever attempted? Including many poorly thought out escapades with Otis?

Tom tucked the bittersweet memories of Otis aside and set his eyes on the large, perfect white door, and knocked.

In the span of minutes it took for the butler to come to the door, Tom lived and died a thousand times. Or so it seemed in his soul. For this was an errand of the heart.

The graying, slender black man answered the door. What had Lauren said his name was? Abraham?

Tom managed a smile for the man. "Good day, Abraham."

There was only a slight upturn of his mouth. Barely perceptible, but there.

Clearing his throat, Tom straightened his father's only Sunday jacket. Tom had dressed in his own best trousers and shirt, but he did not have a jacket. Only a coat. And while it was too warm for that, a visit like this called for the best he could manage.

Still, this butler was dressed better than he.

"I would like to speak with Mr. Crawford."

Abraham's eyes widened. Again, only slightly. The man seemed to try his best not to portray any emotion. He stared at Tom for a few moments. Was he considering whether to honor Tom's request?

At length, Abraham stepped back and opened the door wider. "This way, sir."

Tom stepped into the house for the first time. The entry was as large as the Amoses' entire house. Everything appeared clean and bright, nearly blinding in its brilliance. Much different than the home in which he was raised with its wooden walls, earthen floors, and humble décor of browns and oranges. This home, however, was full of whites and blues, tiles, marble, and other fine materials.

"This way." Abraham's voice rose as he repeated himself.

Jerking his head in that direction, Tom realized he had become distracted. He picked up step behind Abraham.

They moved down a hall and into another large room. Was this the family parlor? Deep burgundy carpet covered the floor and fine curtains allowed the light to shimmer as it entered the room. The dark wood of the furniture was offset by burgundy and cream patterned padding.

Abraham held out an arm toward the room.

Tom entered, worrying about the traces of dirt on his boots.

The door closed behind him.

He whirled around. Had Abraham left him in here? Alone?

Turning in the space, Tom became less sure what to do with himself. Should he sit? That didn't seem right. Nor did it seem suitable for him to stand awkwardly at the entrance to the room.

Would Mr. Crawford come here? If so, he might come in to find Tom standing here gawking at the oversized space that could hold most of the rooms in his father's house. No, he didn't want that.

Stepping further into the parlor, he moved to the piano. The only piano he had ever seen was the older one at the church. He had never laid eyes on one so grand. It was as big as two dining tables.

Reaching forth, he touched one of the white keys. Smooth. His finger slid easily across the surface. The black keys shone in the sunlight coming through the nearby window. Laying his hand over the collection of black and white, side by side, he marveled at the instrument. Could he produce harmony from it? Could Lauren?

The door opened.

He looked up and his hand pressed down. The piano betrayed his snooping with a loud sound.

Mr. Crawford's gaze landed on Tom. A frown shown the man's displeasure.

Tom withdrew his hand and stood straight, muttering an apology.

Crawford waved it off. Was he already bored with the interruption in his day? This did not bode well for Tom. The older man strode into the room and toward a chair near the window. Then he sat and looked at Tom.

"What can I do for you? Your tenancy has only just begun. What situation could possibly have arisen that requires my attention?" Mr. Crawford pinned Tom with steel eyes.

Tom licked his lips. "There are no problems with the tenancy." Coming around the piano, he then stood several feet away from Lauren's father.

Crawford's brows furrowed. "Then what can I help you with?"

Tom played with the fabric at the corner of the jacket opening. Then forced his hands to still and fall at his sides. He could do this.

Taking in a deep breath, he pushed it out and said what he came to. "Mr. Crawford, I know I am of little means. And I am not what you probably envisioned for your daughter. But I will do everything I can to take care of her and provide for her. I would like to ask permission to court your daughter, sir."

"With the intention of marriage?"

Tom nodded, leg working a nervous pump.

Crawford's features twisted into something Tom had a difficult time distinguishing. He stood. "You? What could you possibly offer my daughter in the way of comfort? Stability?"

"I can offer her love."

The man scoffed at that, walking toward the window. "Love. What does anyone have need of love?

Tom opened his mouth but was cut off by a wave of Crawford's hand as he turned his back to Tom.

"Now be gone. I've had enough of this headache for today."

What could Tom say? What could he do? He wanted to plead with the man, to speak his piece. But there were no words that could be used to convince such a man.

Looking at Crawford's back, he nodded, though the man couldn't see it. "Sorry for the disturbance."

Crawford remained stoic, eyes trained out the window.

Tom spun and made his way out of the parlor, down the hall, and was quickly out of the mansion altogether. How could he ever think such a thing was possible?

Lauren leaned over her okra. They would be wonderful in a stew. And it was almost time to pick them. Any day now.

The front door slammed. She heard it from her garden. Who had left the house in such a huff? Looking up from her plants, she searched to the right and left side of the house, watching for whomever it was to come into view.

She shrugged.

Perhaps they had gone toward the main road. Turning back to her work, she moved to the patch beyond the vines. It would be time for the strawberries soon. Lauren could hardly wait. Strawberry pie!

Standing, she stepped to the edge of the garden. Movement to the left caught her eye. A figure walked with hurried steps in the direction of the creek.

Was that? Tom?

Narrowing her eyes to focus her vision, she tried to take in more details. It had to be him!

Had he come to see her? Did her father send him away? Was that why the door slammed? Lifting the hem of her skirt, she took off after him.

Holding her hat to keep it on her head, she moved as quickly as her skirt would allow, but his longer legs carried him away faster.

"Tom!"

The wind blew in her direction, muffling her words. What drove him to retreat at such a pace? Would he never pause to catch his breath? She needed to do so.

"Tom!"

She prayed he would hear her. As it was, his figure became smaller and smaller. Soon disappearing across the field and into the small clump of trees around the creek.

Should she let him go? Halting, she bent in half to draw in air. If only she wasn't wearing this cursed corset! She couldn't breathe properly.

Her heart pounded as she looked toward the creek. She couldn't give up now. Somehow, deep down, she knew he needed her.

Groaning, she bit at her lip and pushed through the painful stitch in her side. As she neared the creek, she shifted her path to make for the shallow part where the rocks created a way across.

But something gave her pause. Holding her breath, she listened. The gentle tumble of the water over the small stones welcomed her. But there was another sound.

Plop.

Yes, there it was.

Plop.

Where was that coming from?

Plop.

She strained her ears. To the right. It couldn't be more than fifteen or so feet away.

Stepping back onto the grassy field, she moved around the trees until she spotted him.

Tom sat on the bank, jacket discarded and lying beside him. His back to her, he picked up small rocks at random, throwing them into the water.

"Tom?" She kept her voice gentle and her tone soft, not wanting to startle him.

He jerked around, eyes wide. Spotting her, his shoulders relaxed, but his eyes fell. Then he turned toward the creek again.

With careful steps, she made her way to him. It wouldn't do to twist her ankle on the uneven ground.

Now at Tom's side, she stood for a moment, gazing down at him even as he kept his eyes on the water. Then she shifted her attention to the stream as well.

"You're a difficult man to catch."

"Am I?" There was no hint of humor in his voice.

She knelt next to him, putting a hand on his shoulder. "Why were you in such a hurry?"

Nothing.

"Please, Tom." Lauren rubbed his arm as she settled onto her hip, laying her legs to the side. "Talk to me."

Tom sat on his backside, knees in front of his chest with his arms folded on top. He shifted his focus to her then, meeting her eyes. But said nothing.

"Did my father send you away?"

He turned forward, examining his hands, intertwining his fingers.

"My father doesn't say who I can and can't see."

Tom made a strange noise. A little like a snort.

"Tom, talk to me." Lauren put both of her hands on his arm nearest to her.

"I don't know what to say." His eyes met hers.

"Tell me what happened."

"Your father doesn't think I'm good enough."

Lauren furrowed her brows. "What does it matter what he thinks? I think you're more than—"

"He won't let me court you."

Her eyes widened. "Court me?" She had not guessed he would do such a thing. Did Tom truly feel that way about her?

Tom's eyes softened and he captured her hands in his, angling his body toward hers. "Yes, Lauren, I want to court you, to marry you. So much."

Lauren's heart expanded. Would it explode? But then...her father had refused Tom. What did that mean?

"But we can't do anything. Not without your father's blessing." He started to turn away.

She grabbed at the collar of his shirt, catching a fistful. "That doesn't seem fair."

Tom's hands fell on her arms, his thumbs soothing her with small movements. "It's the way things are."

"But…" She caught herself. Dare she speak what was in her heart? Biting at her lip, Lauren gazed into his deep brown eyes. And she couldn't stop herself. "I love you."

His lips spread into a smile. "And I love you." One of his hands came to rest on the side of her face. "But that's not enough."

"Why not?" Moisture filled her eyes.

He shrugged. "It's just not."

Tears stung as they fell.

Tom gathered her to his chest.

And as she cried, Lauren began to form a plan. This would not be the end for them.

Parting with Lauren had been one of the more difficult things he had ever done. Doing so without pressing his lips to hers had been even more so. But he didn't want to take that next step. Not if they would not be wed. It wouldn't be right, kissing a woman who would not be his wife.

A yawn forced its way out as he neared his father's farm. A good night's sleep would be refreshing. If he could sleep. Rest had eluded him these last several nights. Would Lauren's declaration of love allow him to find it now?

Yet for all their affection for one another, what did it mean? There was naught they could do about it. He could not whisk her away. Her father had been right. How could Tom provide any manner of comfortable life for her?

His dream of going west, of escaping this place and these memories seemed hopeless at best. Most likely just plain foolish. Who was he to drag Lauren along on these boyish fantasies? Perhaps it was best her father stood his ground.

Reaching for the door's latch, Tom realized he had not

been bowled over by Jeremiah and Josephine. They couldn't still be busy with chores. And it was yet early for dinner.

He pulled the door open and stepped inside the cozy living space. The aroma of Ma's dumplings greeted him. Closing his eyes, he soaked it in.

But only for a moment.

"The prodigal son returns." Pa smiled from his seat at the table.

Why was Pa in so early? Shouldn't he be out minding the animals? But there he was, plain as day, sipping coffee.

The older farmer stood and closed the distance to his son. He laid a weathered hand on Tom's shoulder. "Ma told me you borrowed my jacket. I can only imagine what for. Girl, is it?"

Tom's gaze fell to the floor as he nodded. There was no reason to hide it from his father.

"Aren't you one for secrets?" Pa moved to the stove and poured more coffee from the pot warming on the burner.

Giving him a sideways glance, Tom wondered how much he would have to disclose. How much did he want to share?

Ma stepped into the room from the partitioned off bed space. "I declare, those two troublemakers will be the death of me!"

Tom shifted his eyes toward her. "What are they doing now?"

"The usual. Chasing chickens and scaring the milk cows. It's a wonder how we get anything to produce around here. I set them out by the barn to snap peas."

Tom winced. Ma's favorite punishment. Of course, snapping the peas had to be done. But it was such a mindless chore that she reserved it for...special occasions.

Ma caught Tom's eyes, brows raised. "How did it go?"

Pa arched a brow.

"The meeting didn't go as well as I hoped." Tom stepped

back as Ma passed in front of him, making her way to the dish cabinet and pulling down plates.

She handed them to Tom. "No? Well, no matter. You're a fine farmer whether Mr. Crawford sees it or not."

"You had a meeting with Mr. Crawford?" Pa coughed. Had he sipped too fast? Choked on his coffee? Perhaps Tom wasn't the only one of the Matthews men intimidated by Mr. Crawford.

"Yes. But it wasn't like that." Tom sighed. Maybe it was time to tell them the truth. "It's not what you think."

Ma turned her head from her position at the stove, stirring dinner.

Pa paused mid-sip, setting his cup down.

Tom set the dishes on the table and leaned on the back of a chair.

"Perhaps you should tell us what all of this *is* about." Pa's voice was calm, but firm.

Nodding, Tom pulled out the chair and landed in its seat.

Ma stepped hesitantly to the table. She slid into the seat next to Pa, across from Tom.

Placing hands on the table, Tom examined them before raising his face to catch his parents' gazes. There was no better way than to just come out with it. "I went to ask him for his daughter's hand."

Pa's mouth twitched.

Ma frowned.

"It wasn't supposed to happen. I didn't intend for it to. But it just did. We met one day...the day Clementine died. Then I saw her again at the Amos home..."

Ma's eyes widened.

They wouldn't understand. How could they?

Tom looked away. "It all must seem strange to you." Then he caught their eyes again, each in turn. "But I love her."

They continued to watch Tom, as if waiting for him to continue.

"But Mr. Crawford refused me. And I would do the same in his shoes. I don't know what I thought. Who would give their daughter to a man who has nothing to his name but a dream and only a few dollars to get him there?"

Tom pushed back from the table and crossed his arms, looking at the floor. "How am I supposed to take her away from all this if I can't free myself?" He stole a glance in their direction.

They exchanged a long look.

Ma nodded.

Pa stood and walked to the partitioned off bedroom.

"I know you two don't want me to leave. You think I'm foolish to want to do anything but what I was raised to. But I believe I can have a better life out west. There is opportunity for anyone who will dare take it."

In the next moment, Pa loomed over Tom. He held his hand out, holding a stack of bills wrapped in a brown leather binding.

Tom looked between his parents. "What is this?"

"Take it." Pa nudged Tom's shoulder with the money. "It's for you. Your mother took on some folks' laundry and mending, and the hogs had a good litter this year. We knew you would need it."

Not sure what else to do, Tom held out his hand to receive the precious gift. "I...I don't understand."

Pa walked away, circling the table, and returning to his seat.

"Your Pa and I may not understand, but we will always believe in you." Ma's eyes were glassy.

Was it just Tom's imagination or did Pa sniffle?

Perhaps it was Tom's emotion that welled in that moment.

"But I can't take—"

"You can." Pa turned on Tom. "You must. It's the only way."

Tom pressed the bundle with his other hand. The only way. Yes, there was a way. But dare he take it?

Stepping into the oversized entryway, Lauren smiled to herself. The warmth of Tom's embrace still lingered. And the skin of her forehead tingled where his lips had pressed a farewell kiss. How she had wanted him to truly kiss her. Why did he hold back?

But he was a gentleman and pulled away after the simple contact that affected her more than she would have imagined possible.

Moving toward the stairs, she sighed.

"You are not to see that boy again." The voice was gruff, coming from the shadows at the doorway to the far hall.

Lauren paused, foot already on the first step. She didn't have to look in that direction to know it was her father.

"I will not suffer this humiliation." His voice was stern.

Removing her hand from the banister, Lauren faced the darkened figure. "You cannot cage me forever, Father."

He stepped into the fading light of day streaming in through the window. His features twisted into an angry grimace. "Do not forget yourself, young lady. You are *my* daughter. And as long as you wish to live under the protection of my name, you will do as I say."

Lauren met, and held, his stony gaze. There would come a day when she would have to stand up to this man. Had that day come? She swallowed against an impossibly dry mouth and opened her lips to speak.

Nothing came.

She dropped her head, looking to the floor. Why couldn't

she say her piece to him? Tell him she cared not for his position nor this fine house?

His features relaxed. "You may be excused." Pa turned and moved toward the hall leading to the family parlor. "Please prepare for dinner. I don't want your mother to be embarrassed by your dress."

Her face warmed. *Say something. Speak your heart!* "I will take dinner in my room."

He spun. His eyes hard on her once more. After a few moments, he nodded. "As you wish. But remember what I said."

Biting at her lip, she looked at the lowering sun outside the window. The clipping of his shoes on the floor let her know he had moved off down the hall.

Once the sound faded, she whirled and raced up the stairs.

What cowardice! How could she face Tom again? Could she not stand up to her father for her heart? For the man she loved? She was hopeless.

Jerking her door open, she slammed it for good measure. Then flung herself upon her bed. What would become of her and Tom? The plan that had begun to form in her mind, a dangerous plan indeed, seemed to lose form and substance in the face of her timidity. It could not be done.

God, I need Your strength. I need Tom...to be with him. I know he will care for me. I know we can make a life together. And I know I need to be free of my father. But I am powerless to do so. Give me strength. Give me wisdom.

As she prayed, Lauren was filled anew with determination. And she knew what she had to do.

Chapter Five

Where could she be? Dare he venture to the manor house again? Would her father banish him from the property? End his tenancy for good? Did it matter?

Tom had not seen Lauren in four days. Rather unusual on the face of it, but all the more heart-wrenching after their declarations to one another. And he became fearful of what her father might have done. How far would he go to ensure Tom and Lauren wouldn't see one another?

Having talked himself into and out of barging up to the mansion several times now, he sat on the edge of his allotted land, stuck in a moment of indecision.

No, he could not tarry. He had to do it. Regardless of the risks. She needed him.

Rising, he made his way toward the looming house. He could have counted the yards to the front door, but they seemed immeasurable today, dragging out in front of him.

As he neared, he saw a horse-drawn carriage, prepared and sitting in front of the house. Was Crawford sending Lauren away?

Tom picked up his step, arriving at the small porch as Mr. Crawford emerged from the house, Abraham in tow. Crawford spoke hurriedly to the man. Perhaps giving him instructions.

Abraham spotted Tom. His eyes widened. Did he wish to warn Tom? He did not betray Tom's arrival, but his altered focus alerted Crawford to another's presence.

Crawford turned in Tom's direction and then his eyes narrowed. He halted. "Mr. Matthews."

Tom closed the distance between them.

"What can I do for you?" The older man spoke through clenched teeth.

"I want to speak with Lauren."

"She is no concern of yours." Crawford shoved his hands into gloves as if Tom were nothing more than a minor annoyance. "And if I were you, I would spend my time worrying after my farm. If you have one after today." He arched a brow toward Tom.

"I just want to know that she is all right."

"I have said what I will on this matter." Crawford stepped into the carriage. "Abraham, will you see this farmer off my property?"

"But, I—" Tom asserted.

"We will speak about your tenancy tomorrow. As you see, I have business to attend to right now. Good day, Mr. Matthews."

With that, Crawford nodded at the coachman and the man slapped the reins. The horses took off, and Tom could do nothing but watch the carriage circle the dirt path in front of the manor house and drive off into the distance.

Abraham put a hand on his arm. "Mr. Matthews, please don't make this more difficult."

Tom nodded, holding up a hand. "I'll be on my way."

He sensed Abraham's eyes on him as he took the steps that would carry him farther from Lauren.

Once he was several feet from the house, the door shut. Was there still a chance he might see her? Could she be in her garden?

He glanced over his shoulder.

Abraham was nowhere in sight.

Altering his course, he moved to the back of the house. In a few minutes, the garden came into view.

There was no one in sight. Indeed, the garden appeared as if it had not been tended in days.

Tom frowned. Had she not been allowed outside at all?

Sensing eyes on him, he glanced up. There, at the window, he spotted Abraham, watching him. The man gave him a stern look.

Tom nodded and moved off toward his own apportioned land. His heart fell, his opportunity lost.

As he neared his tenant farm, his thoughts turned briefly to his work. What was the point? If Crawford were to end his tenancy tomorrow, was there any reason to continue? He made short work of putting away his tools. There was nowhere for him to go but back to his father's farm.

What now? There was no Lauren. No farm. No way to see his dream come to fruition. Though, without Lauren, did he even want that dream now? Or had it, just like the world, lost its color, its appeal?

Nearing the creek, he found the embankment where he and Lauren had sat not one week prior and shared words of love with each other. Such a tender memory.

Plopping down, he plucked a few strands of grass and let them fall from his grasp.

A rustle behind gave him pause. He held his breath.

"You're a difficult man to catch."

He jerked around, rising at the same time. Closing the distance between them, Lauren was in his arms in a moment. Tom held her as if he would never let go. Indeed, he never wanted to.

"Are you well?" he spoke into her shoulder.

"Yes," she whispered.

He pulled back to look into her eyes. "I can't. I can't be without you."

Her fingers grazed the side of his face. "I know."

"But I don't know how, Lauren. I'm so sorry. I wish I had a way to—"

She placed a finger on his lips.

He quieted.

"I have a plan."

His eyes caught hers. Whatever it was, he would do it... anything to be with her.

"We must elope."

Anything but that. His hands came between them. "Lauren, we can't. Do you know what that would mean? How that would look? I don't want that for you."

She grasped his hands. "I don't care. I have to be with you. And you heard my father—he won't allow it. He's kept me holed up in the house these last four days. If it wasn't for your argument distracting Abraham, I couldn't have snuck out."

"He will find us."

"We have to take that chance. And if he does, hopefully it will be too late."

Tom lowered his head.

"I will die if I stay here, caged like a bird, forced to marry someone I don't love. I want *you*. I want to go west. To find *our* future. To find *our* dreams."

Our dreams. Dare he hope that she wanted what he did? It was true that she didn't want this life. And the west offered a new life, a different life. A life he could give her. A life he so badly wanted to give her.

"Say you'll take me away from all of this. And let me be with you. Always." She gazed up at him, her hazel eyes pleading, so full of love. How could he deny her anything? Much less something that he wanted too?

He freed a hand and took her chin, tilting it ever so slightly.

Her eyes closed.

Tom could no longer resist what his whole being had been crying out for. He lowered his head and pressed his lips to hers.

The contact was simple at first. Sweet. But soon left him wanting. And she responded to his request, opening her lips and inviting deeper contact.

It was bliss. She was heavenly.

When he did pull back, reluctantly, he was certain he floated.

She clung to his shirt, leaning on him.

He wrapped his arms around her, enveloping her in an embrace that grounded him once again.

Could they do this? How could he not?

What does one take when eloping? When you leave all you have known behind and take on a new way of being? A new life?

Lauren's gowns and fine dresses would not suit her anymore. Not out west and not tonight. They would be too conspicuous.

What other option did she have? She had to look into Grace's things. If only she could have asked Mammy to help her. But that would not have served her well. Mammy shouldn't be responsible for that knowledge if she were to be asked. So Lauren would have to do it on her own.

Mammy slept when Lauren sneaked into her room. Grace's trunk sat in the corner, undisturbed since the day... since a few years past.

Lauren's hands shook as she worked the latch on the trunk. In truth, it was not much more than a painted crate. But it was all Mammy could afford to remember her daughter by.

The lid creaked as Lauren raised it. Glancing over at Mammy's resting form, she worried the older woman would stir. Then she relaxed. Mammy was a hard sleeper.

Lauren held her hands to her chest. Dare she reach in? These were Grace's few earthly possessions. Would touching them be like disturbing her grave? Such a thought was nonsense. This was no time for such superstitions.

With trembling fingers, she grazed the garments at the top. The clothes were soft, not because of the fabric, but because of how many times they had been worn and washed. Grace hadn't had many things to her name.

Lauren pulled out a gray dress. She remembered Grace wearing this one, though the memory, like the pattern, was fading. Would she lose her memories of Grace altogether in the years to come? That thought stung.

She shook her head. There wasn't time for her to fall apart. One more garment remained. Then she would leave Grace's things, and Mammy, in peace.

Pulling out Grace's only other dress, a brown one, Lauren closed the trunk. As much as she had wanted to delve into the past and peruse the precious contents of the large memory box, she dared not.

Rising, she held the dresses to herself, praying her flight would be more successful than Grace's.

Lauren paused by Mammy's bed. Could she leave without a farewell to the woman who had been as a mother to her? But how could she give her a proper goodbye?

Stepping around the small bed that somehow fit Mammy and Abraham, Lauren leaned over the woman's head and pressed a gentle kiss to her forehead.

The woman shifted.

Lauren held her breath and pulled the dresses behind her back.

Mammy's eyes opened. "Sweet child, what you doing up at this hour?"

"I've come to kiss you good night."

Mammy smiled. "You're a good child to this ole' mammy, Laurie-belle."

Lauren pulled the covers to Mammy's chin and patted her shoulder.

The older woman turned to the wall and slipped back into unconsciousness.

Lauren tiptoed out of the room, pausing at the door. "Good night, Mammy. You've been good to this little girl." A tear escaped and made a trail down Lauren's face. She wiped it away. This was what she had to do.

Moving down the hall to her own room, Lauren exchanged her dress for Grace's gray one. Ma should retire soon and then it would be time. She would meet Tom by the creek in due time and, with any luck, they could make it to the next county before Pa returned home tomorrow morning.

A wave of excitement passed through her. And nausea followed. Would they make it? Or would their plan fall apart?

They would. God was on their side. And they would overcome whatever obstacles stood in their way.

Lauren watched the sun dip below the horizon. And listened for her mother and the servants to stop moving about the halls.

Once the house was quiet, she waited one hour longer. Which was one hour longer than she preferred. For in that time, she imagined every possible thing that could go wrong.

But she also dreamed of how perfect their life would be. The west—a place of freedom from slavery, from the remnants of the war, from her parents. Yes, it was worth the risk.

Opening her door but a crack, she peered out. All was still and dark. She gathered her bundle—the other dress and her underthings. A light burden to bear. Should she gather food-stuffs from the kitchen? No, that would only increase the chance of getting caught.

Lauren slipped out of her room. Moving soundlessly down the hall, she made her way to the servants' stairs. Just a few more moments and she would be out of the house.

She stood at the servants' exit to the outside and took in the manor house once more. From this perspective, the house was quite different. The fine whites and burgundies were not present, it was simple wood grains and white paint—a mimicry of the more extravagant parts of the house. An echo of the grandeur of the home she had always known.

Nevermore. This would no longer be her home. Her place was with Tom. That's where her home would be—with him.

Lauren reached for the door latch, sucked in a breath, and pulled.

A hand grabbed her arm.

She gasped, spinning to face her captor, and found herself looking into the deep soulful eyes of Abraham.

He spoke not a word, but his hand on her arm was firm.

"Please, Abraham. You know what he's like. Don't stop me."

"I don't want you to do anything you'll regret."

Lauren placed a gentle hand on Abraham's, which loos-ened its grip on her. "I love him."

Abraham's eyes were sad. Were his thoughts on Grace?

"I have to try. I will make it. For me, and for Grace."

His hand fell to his side.

She touched his shoulder. "All will be well. You'll see."

Abraham frowned, but reached out to hold the door open.

Lauren wanted to say something further, but there were no words that would assuage his fears. So she nodded and forced a smile onto her features that she didn't feel. Then she stepped down and into the night, only looking back once.

Abraham remained in the doorway, his form silhouetted in the night. How long would he watch after her?

It was no matter. Tom waited by the creek. She would be with him in a few moments. And then, their future awaited.

Chapter Six

Tom's gaze was trained on the hillside in the direction of the manor house. What were they doing? This was crazy. Was there the slimmest possibility they'd make it? How had he convinced himself this would work?

He had said his farewells to his parents but had not been able to speak goodbyes to Josephine and Jeremiah. Ma and Pa decided it would be best if they didn't know until tomorrow. That didn't keep him from giving them an extra hug—or two—at bedtime.

This venture would not have been possible without his parents. Not only had they given him the money they had saved, but Pa had also procured two horses in secret. As much as Ma wanted to load the horses down with things for him and Lauren, Pa had warned her it would be best if Tom and Lauren traveled light. Still, she packed what she thought they could not live without. Now if only Tom could erase his memory of the worry in Ma's eyes when he'd departed.

But this was what he had to do. For Otis—to live life to the fullest. For Lauren. For them both.

A figure topped the hill. Was it...?

The skirt was not as full and the sleeves were cut closer to her arms, but it was undeniably...his Lauren.

He wanted to run to her, but wisdom stilled his motion forward. It was best he wait under the cover of the trees—a wait that lasted forever.

When she neared, he reached for her and pulled her into his eager embrace. He would never let go of her again.

"Did you have any trouble?" he breathed into her hair.

She shook her head.

He couldn't help himself. His lips found hers and claimed them once, twice, before pulling back.

Lauren smiled at him.

Tom pressed a last kiss to her forehead before tugging her toward the horses. "This is Lady. She'll be a good horse for you."

Lauren hesitated, holding back a step.

"Something amiss?"

"I've never been much of a horsewoman."

Tom's lips angled. "We'll take care of that. Later. For now, perhaps you should ride with me." He reached for her again.

She stopped him with an outstretched arm. Her reluctant movements gave him pause. "It would slow us. The animal bearing the weight of two."

He looked at the two horses. There was little reason in arguing with her. She spoke true.

Her gaze captured his as he turned. "I can ride."

His brow furrowed. "Are you certain?"

She nodded. That brave streak in his darling gave him cause to fill with pride. What a woman God had given him.

Allowing one more slight grin, he murmured, "Trust me and stay close."

Her gaze slid to the looming horse and widened. Still she nodded.

Wishing for more time to acquaint her with the animal, he

gently drew her alongside the mare and hoisted her into the saddle.

She flung her leg over the horse's back and sat astride, like a man. It surprised him.

Her face colored. "I never could get used to the feel of the side-saddle."

Tom averted his gaze from the way her position on the horse exposed a portion of her stocking-clad calves. He turned to his own steed and mounted with ease. "Shall we?"

When he looked back at her, she seemed to be surveying the area around them. Was she saying her own farewell? Then those glittering orbs met his. He found determination there.

And she nodded once more.

He shifted and dug his heels into the horse's flank. The animal took off, giving him good speed. Glancing back, needing to assure himself she was well, he noted that Lauren held her own and even kept up.

Into the night they raced. But it wasn't until sometime later that his trepidations quieted. And not until they reached Benton County did he breathe easier.

That is...until the thundering of hooves sounded in the distance.

The night sky lightened. Or was it just her imagination? Had they truly been riding that long? Were they almost to Camden?

Lauren's heart beat almost as fast as her horse's hooves landed. Were they safe from her father's clutches? That thought brought a growing ache to her chest.

Tom kept looking behind them. What concerned him so?

She tried to even her breathing. Nothing good would come from her worry. As she watched, he veered to the right.

Intent on remaining with him, Lauren pulled on Lady's reins and followed.

They moved through the trees, winding this way and that. Was he searching for something?

A dog howled behind them—a bloodhound. Were they being pursued?

Her pulse thrummed faster and her stomach weighed heavy.

His gaze caught hers. There was steel there. How could he remain so calm? He called out to his horse and urged more speed from the animal.

She, in turn, did the same. Straining her ears, she searched out the thunder of clamoring hooves in pursuit. But the loud thuds of her heart and the vibrations of Lady's stride deafened her to all else. So she kept her eyes on Tom. He would not steer her wrong.

He jerked at something in the distance.

Dragging her gaze from him to the horizon, she saw it too.

Somehow...they were pursued from before and behind.

Tom shifted uneasily as he attempted to direct his mare in a northernly direction.

That wouldn't work. And she knew it.

But she trusted him. She would see this through with him. Come what may.

Though as she tugged on the reins, her horse's steps faltered.

Tom's horse came nearer. But whatever had spooked Lady gave her cause to buck.

Lauren scrambled for a tighter hold. But it wasn't to be had.

The horse's movements became more intense.

"Lauren," Tom yelled, his voice thick with terror.

Her hold slipped and she flew through the air. It was an odd sensation—she became light and floated as the moment stretched. But fear gripped her even as she considered that this was how a feather must feel.

Then she slammed into the earth.

And all went dark.

When Tom saw Lauren's horse attempt to alter its step amidst the stones, he knew there would be trouble. Sure enough, the uneven fall of the hooves, startled the animal into a frenzy.

Time slowed and Tom pressed his horse closer. Could he reach Lauren in time? Could she hold on?

But she was bucked off, her body flailing as if it became one of his sister's rag dolls.

There wasn't even time for her to scream before she smacked into the earth.

And lay still.

He jerked his mount to a halt and jumped down, rushing to her side. "Lauren!"

Her body lay at an odd rest. Nothing could be certain. Was she broken? Would she now be eternally out of reach?

His hands flew over her face, beseeching her to open her eyes. "Lauren!"

The world fell away. Including those whose pursuit had caused this.

No. He had caused this. His desire to have her as his wife. His blasted dreams. And the crazy notion they might be able to escape into the night. The blame lay solely at his feet.

Gently, he leaned down and pressed his forehead to hers as hot tears poured from him. "Lauren, forgive me. Don't leave me. I'm sorry. I can't...can't live without you. Don't make me."

He was only somewhat aware as the contingency of horses surrounded them, encircling them, blocking off all hope.

No. There was something these men didn't know...and could not understand. Tom would never leave this place. Never. He would remain here and now just as assuredly as his heart would. For it belonged with her.

Boots trudged closer. "Lauren!"

The call was an older man. A familiar voice—Mr. Crawford.

But Tom couldn't tear himself from his beloved even long enough to look at the man who sounded genuinely distraught.

Once again, Tom wanted to blame him and his proud prejudiced ways. But there would be no relief in doing so.

Hands gripped Tom's shoulders and pulled him away.

He fought the men grabbing at him. And how he did so. With everything that was in him.

But it was no use. They were too many and too strong. He was dragged away from Lauren's body.

Mr. Crawford fell to his knees beside her, leaning over her a moment, then pulling back. "I didn't realize. I never knew... how did I not know?" The man's despair mirrored Tom's own. How was that possible?

"What have you done?" The older man's eyes flashed back at Tom as he glared over his shoulder. "Do you realize you might have killed her?"

Tom continued to struggle. "I...I can't..."

"Can't what? Can't gain your grip on sanity?" Mr. Crawford huffed. "I should have you drawn and quartered."

Not that it mattered. Everything emptied out of Tom. His future was but a dark shadow without her to light it. *God, how could this be Your way?*

Wait...

Did Mr. Crawford say he *might* have...? Did that mean Lauren was...?

He tried to free himself enough to shift and peer around Mr. Crawford, who turned back to his daughter.

"Daffodil, I'll take care of you. I always do."

"No," she groaned.

It was weak and it was mumbled, but it was sure.

"Lauren," Tom called, not caring as tears pricked his eyes and rough hands held him painfully in place. "Lauren!'

Mr. Crawford slid a hand under Lauren's back and raised her upper body. There wasn't much Tom could see as Mr. Crawford was in the way.

Tom ached...no, burned...to know that she was well and not horribly broken. He couldn't stand the idea that she was hurt in any way.

But the men restraining him wouldn't turn him lose. Not even an inch. Had they no pity?

Lauren raised a hand to her father. It offered blessed hope that she would be all right.

"Don't move, darling. And don't try to talk. We'll see this scoundrel is dealt with." Mr. Crawford turned back to Tom. And there was murder in his eyes.

Lauren hurt all over. Everywhere. But her awareness of both the pain and the movements around her increased. Her father leaned over her and...where was Tom? He called for her, but she couldn't place him. It was yet too dim to make out much beyond Pa's face in the light of the few lanterns that surrounded them.

"Pa..." she managed. "Wh-where is Tom?"

"Never mind that, Daffodil," Pa crooned. "You'll be right as rain."

"No." She pushed at his hold. "I won't go back with you. No matter what you do." She forced her legs to move and she kicked, gaining some distance from her father.

"Be still," Mr. Crawford commanded. "You will mind yourself and do as I say."

"Or what?" Lauren used every ounce of strength to rise.

Despite the protests of her father and...Tom?

She continued to search him out. There, in a group of men. Were her father's men holding Tom prisoner? Did Pa intend to string him up? Or just shoot him outright?

Moving toward him, she stumbled and nearly fell, but sucked in a ragged breath and kept going. Until she came closer to Tom.

He pressed against his captors to try and reach her. "Don't. Do as your father bids. You'll be safe."

As if she only cared about herself. Did he not realize that without him, all of her dreams, her very heart, would shrivel?

One of Mr. Crawford's men stepped between her and Tom, preventing her from getting to him. The man brandished a rifle...as if his looming presence wasn't enough.

She turned back toward Pa and her vision swirled. After a moment to brace herself, she glared at him. "What will you do, Pa? Shoot me the way you shot Grace?"

Silence filled the air.

Pa opened his mouth, but nothing came forth.

"Am I nothing more than that to you? A possession? Chattel?"

She prepared for his ire, for his anger to burn at her words. But as her voice rose, his face became difficult to discern.

"What will it be, Father?"

He turned away from her and lowered his head.

She scanned the men. "Shame. Shame on all of you! Attacking an unarmed man and woman."

Turning in a circle that made her vision worse, she moved about to watch her father.

His shoulders slumped and a hand went to his face. What was this?

Pa spun toward her, his face a mask and his gun in hand by his side.

"I wish it didn't have to come to this." His voice, once laced with anger, was now timid.

"Come to what? You dirtying your hands again?" She stepped toward him. The rumbling sound behind warned that Tom strove for freedom once more. To protect her from her father?

No. She was done hiding...behind him, behind propriety and manners, behind Grace's memory, behind everything the man abhorred. She would face him.

Pa stopped advancing. He looked to the ground...and nodded. When he met Lauren's gaze again, there was something almost sad in his eyes.

"All my life," Pa said, his voice breaking. "I worked to create a legacy. And I wanted to pass it on to you, to secure your comfort. It never occurred to me that you would want no part of it."

Lauren looked away because, despite everything, she was still unable to watch her father's pained expression. She held her ground, however.

"But you are all that will be left of me in the world. And tonight, I thought I had lost you. Most assuredly as I breathe, I believed you were gone."

Her heart softened at the edges, but only just.

"It is a shame indeed that it takes something like nearly losing everything to make a man consider his life. And find it wanting."

She ached to ease his anguish and speak some words of compassion. But they wouldn't come. He was right. He had made horrid decisions. Had brought great pain on many people. In the name of what society said was well enough. But in her heart, she had always known it was not.

Pa sighed. "I have...done things. Things I can't undo and

things I will regret for the rest of my life." He gazed at her. "But I never wanted your future to be one of them."

The older man looked between her and Tom.

"Release him." The words were gruff, a remnant of the man she knew. But different, somehow.

She turned in time to see Tom being thrust forward.

He stumbled and nearly lost his footing, but he soon gained his gait and rushed to her. Then gathered her in his arms, seemingly uncaring of her father's presence.

His arms were more solid than expected and...wonderful. Especially considering all that had happened in these last several moments. And as she had been certain to never feel his embrace again.

Pa cleared his throat.

Lauren turned, but did not release Tom. She wasn't about to let her father work any manner of ill on him.

But there was a sheen in Pa's eyes. And his features fell. By all appearances, he was a man crushed by the weight of his choices. And their consequences.

He couldn't change them now. Nor could she. No matter how she wished them to be righted.

"I want you to be well. And I don't want to trap you in a loveless marriage." There was a thick undercurrent in Pa's voice. As if he knew that situation all too well. "You deserve to be loved. You deserve to be happy." Pa's voice hitched on the last word.

Lauren met his eyes.

He approached her again, releasing the revolver's hammer and setting it on the ground. "So, no. I will not see you shot. I would see you married."

Pa stopped within arm's length of Lauren.

"To the man of your choosing."

Lauren's breath caught in her throat. "You mean that?"

Pa nodded. "Please..." Pa choked on the word. "Please, Daffodil. Come home. Let me make things right."

Could she trust him? She looked to Tom.

He gave her arm a squeeze and nodded. As if he somehow knew that all would be well.

Lauren turned to her father. "I will, Pa." She moved to him and allowed him to encircle her with an arm.

"I love you, Daffodil. I'm sorry...for so many things."

"Me too, Pa. Me too."

<h1 style="text-align:right">Chapter Seven</h1>

reathe. Just breathe.

Lauren closed her eyes and took a moment for herself.

This was the much anticipated day. It all came down to this one day, this one moment.

Once Lauren stepped into the church, she would be led down the aisle to her groom. Something tingled through her from her core to the edges of her limbs. Nerves? A wave of something akin to excited fear passed through her.

She took another deep breath and let the sensations wash over her.

"Ready?"

Turning, she met Pa's clear blue eyes. The dark storm that once filled those orbs had dissipated. Now there was calm. If only she could partake of it for this day.

Pa took her hand and looped it around his arm, smiling. "Tom is waiting."

Yes, Tom. Her beloved. That was who stood at the other end of that aisle amidst the crowd of faces. Tom.

"We best not keep him waiting any longer." Lauren

offered her father a smile from the swell of emotion within her.

Patting her hand, he nodded to the manservant at the door. The young man opened it, revealing the small gathering beyond.

The tune that heralded her entrance commenced and all eyes were on her.

But hers were fixed on Tom. She would never forget the look on his face in that moment—his adoration and appreciation were evident. As was the fight to hold back his more tender emotions.

She was overwhelmed by the force of his love for her. All of her...for who she was, not for her name or her place in society. But just *her*.

And he stood at the ready to receive her. That was all that mattered.

Moments later, she stood beside Tom. Her father spoke his part of the ceremony and then Tom reached for her.

As their hands connected and they said their vows, Lauren pledged her heart to the man next to her. She would forever put her past behind her and look to a future all theirs.

The ceremony came to a close. Lauren and Tom were wed. Nothing could keep them apart now.

Tom glanced at his bride beside him, etching into his memory the way she looked this day. Would he be able to remember the details of the dress? Perhaps not, but he was certain he would never forget her smile, the way her eyes lit up, or the inflection of her voice when she promised to be his for all their days.

Squeezing her hand drew her eyes to his. A smile graced her lips. They had done the impossible, and against such odds.

He leaned toward her, pressing a kiss to the side of her face. "Can I get you anything?"

She sighed. Did his breath in her ear affect her so?

Tom pulled back enough to watch her features.

Something played across her face, something difficult to describe. Yet it warmed his core.

"Perhaps something to drink?"

He nodded before lifting her gloved hand to his lips. Then he reluctantly slipped away and toward the refreshment table.

Pouring a glass of punch, Tom intended to rejoin Lauren as soon as possible. A clap on his shoulder interrupted his plans.

Tom spun toward the intrusion.

Mr. Crawford stood beside him, grabbing for a glass.

Clearing his throat, Tom stood as tall as he could manage and angled his body toward the man. "Mr. Crawford, I wanted to thank you for everything you've done."

Crawford's gaze landed on Tom. "I've done a lot of wrong things in my life. A lot to regret. I didn't want my daughter to be one of them."

Tom nodded. "That means a lot to me."

"But don't think you are free of me. I will be watching. Someway, somehow. Know that I am."

What did that mean? Did Crawford not trust him to be faithful? To care for her? A fury ignited within, but he quelled it. There would be no reason in it. For Lauren's sake, it would be best if everyone got along.

Tom glanced at Lauren, speaking with a couple of ladies her age. And he spotted her mother doing the same, but she blotted at her eyes with her handkerchief, as if she were in mourning.

"I wish things could be better between Lauren and her mother." Had he said that out loud?

Crawford's gaze turned toward his wife. "That will take time."

Tom nodded. Why had he spoken out? He didn't want to have this conversation with Crawford. "That it may. But with us headed west, their time may have run out."

Crawford met Tom's eyes once again, eyebrow arched. "Matthews, time is all you have."

With that, Crawford took his glass and walked off.

Tom looked after him.

"Did you need help?" a voice broke into his thoughts.

Turning, Tom saw that Lauren had found him at the punch bowl. "Sorry, I got distracted."

Lauren glanced in the direction of her retreating father. "I can see that. Everything all right?"

Tom placed a hand on her arm. "Do not worry."

"I just want everything to work out."

Tom rubbed her arms. "It has, my love, it has. Our very own happily ever after."

The wagon was packed and ready to go. Tom's parents were more helpful than Lauren could have imagined. And Pa had been so generous. More so than she would have thought.

But Lauren slipped away from it all. She had one more stop to make. One that she had avoided.

She had to see Millie, Isaac, and Mrs. Amos one last time.

Her heart thundered in her ears as she neared their tiny home. What would become of them? They had lost their only way to make a life as sharecroppers. No one would let land to a woman, even if Mrs. Amos could work the land.

But Lauren had to see them all the same.

Lauren carried a bag of her mother-in-law's carefully thought out provisions. They could do without a few things.

A sack of foodstuffs could mean another week for the Amos family.

Stepping to the door, Lauren knocked gently.

Mere seconds later, Mrs. Amos opened the door. She smiled broadly at Lauren. How was it she could find such a smile in the midst of her hardship?

"Miz Lauren! Millie and Isaac sure have missed you!"

The sound of two sets of feet running for the open door sounded on the thin boards of the home. And the children crashed into their mother from behind, squeezing around her. Had they heard Mrs. Amos say her name?

Lauren crouched to gather the children in her arms. "My, how you have grown!" Her heart ached as she spoke the words. They had grown, but would that continue to be true? Would they be able to develop and grow into everything they could be?

"I missed you!" Millie shouted, putting her hands on Lauren's cheeks.

"I missed you more." Isaac touched her hair.

"Well, I missed you both the most." Lauren sniffed back tears that threatened to come. They would not serve the children. Only confuse them.

"Now, y'all go play." Mrs. Amos shooed them off into the yard.

Lauren watched them bound off into the sunshine. Then she turned back to Mrs. Amos. "I brought these things for you." She handed over the sack.

Mrs. Amos glanced in the bag. "If I didn't know any better, I'd say these are Miz Matthews'."

"They are." Lauren furrowed her brows. How could Mrs. Amos know that?

Mrs. Amos laughed. "Goodness, child. Don't you know? Everybody can tell Miz Matthews' cornbread when they smell it."

Lauren relaxed and let a smile break across her face.

"But I can't take it. I have a mind this was meant for you." Mrs. Amos held the bag out to Lauren.

"No. You need it. The children—"

"Will be just fine." Mrs. Amos smiled. "I appreciate your concern, Miz Lauren, but we'll be fine."

Lauren was no less confused than before. She couldn't stop her questions. "How? How will you make it?"

"Don't you know? Mr. Crawford found me a position cooking at the Abbott manor."

"He what?"

Mrs. Amos laughed again. "I tell you, child, the Lord takes care of those He calls His own."

Lauren could only nod.

"Now you best be on your way if you're going to make any distance by sundown."

"I agree," a voice behind Lauren said.

Lauren didn't have to turn to know that voice. It was her husband.

"Mr. Matthews, come to collect your wife?"

"Yes, ma'am. And to see that you have what you need." Tom stepped up beside Lauren and put an arm around her waist.

"Your wife already tried to give away some of your Mama's cornbread and vegetables."

Tom appeared stricken. "Not Ma's cornbread!"

Lauren smiled. "Indeed."

"Now, I thank y'all for being so concerned, but we'll be fine. The Lord has us in the palm of His hand."

Leaning forward, Lauren hugged the woman she had come to admire so much.

Tom shook Mrs. Amos' hand and then held out an arm for Lauren.

She slipped a hand though the crook of his elbow, and they began the walk back toward the Matthews' farmhouse.

"Do you suppose that's true?" Lauren gazed at the horizon. Midday was upon them.

"What?"

"That we are in the palm of God's hand?"

"That's what the Bible says." Tom pulled her closer.

"Do you believe it? That an Almighty God would care about us as individuals?"

There was a pause. Was Tom considering her question?

"Yes. I do."

Her eyes met his.

"Because He gave me you. He brought us through all these obstacles. And I can find no other explanation for it."

Lauren leaned into his shoulder. It was a nice thought, that God held them close and would continue to hold them tenderly in His care. What sweet reassurance.

And so, arm in arm, they faced the horizon, knowing that God, and their love for each other, would sustain them for whatever the future, *their* future, held.

Keep reading for a preview of the first book in the Cripple Creek Series!

Thank you, dear reader, for for reading along with me! If you enjoyed this story, I would sincerely appreciate if you would submit a review. It would mean so much to me!

To read more about these characters, follow along with the Cripple Creek Series. Find it at:
https://saraturnquist.com/cripple-creek-series/

The stagecoach moved along, bumping and rocking as it went. Trees and other green scenery whisked by the window. Views of mountains and open plains were visible from the seat of the coach, vistas familiar to its occupant. Katherine Matthews was coming home. She returned to Cripple Creek, no longer the scared, unsure teenager who had left to further her education so many years ago with hopes and dreams of a new life in a new place. No, she had matured into a confident young woman who had grown in stature and in beauty. Her hair was no longer the mousy color she always hated, for it had deepened into the same beautiful chestnut brown she had always admired in her mother's appearance. She'd grown out of her awkward teenage features, and was now well regarded among her peers as a rather handsome woman.

Returning to Cripple Creek brought many rather-mixed emotions to the surface. Imagine, one of her first postings would be at the same schoolhouse where she received her educational start. When her mother wrote to her of the interim need, she was glad to help out. What an odd coincidence that the letter would find her, too, in transition. Would this turn into a permanent placement? Did she want it to?

The mountain scenery became more recognizable, and she thought back on her childhood. There were so many happy times here. Unbidden, her mind wandered to the day of the great tragedy that had marred her spirit—the day Ellie Mae died.

Even all these years later, she carried the scar in her heart. The events of that day had left her broken. Why must thoughts of Ellie Mae plague her so? And all the more as her return became imminent? She shivered as the images from her nightmares the previous evening flitted across her mind. They would not stop. These same visions visited her in sleep night after night. All the more frequently these last weeks.

Closing her eyes, the hazy images took form and became memory. It was as if no time had passed. She and Ellie, walking through the schoolyard just as they did every other day . . .

Hooking arms with Ellie Mae, Katherine stepped out of the schoolhouse and into the yard. A rather large group of students gathered off to the right near the old tree. It didn't bother Katherine. She turned her attention toward the path that would lead home.

"What do you think they're up to?" Ellie Mae whispered.

Katherine glanced in that direction and noticed Betsy Callaway at the center, flapping her jaws. Why would anyone listen to anything she said? But they did. The class at large seemed to adore Betsy. It didn't make sense. Clenching her teeth, Katherine grabbed for Ellie Mae's hand. "Whatever it is, we don't want to be involved." She pulled Ellie Mae along as she walked on, trying to pass the gathering.

"I know Miss Matthews couldn't do it," Betsy said loudly.

Katherine froze in her tracks. What had she just said?

The crowd of students parted and glared at Katherine and Ellie Mae.

"Let's keep going," Ellie Mae pleaded, tugging on Katherine's hand.

She should listen to Ellie Mae and not become a part of whatever game Betsy played. But she could not let Betsy get the best of her. What would everyone think of her?

So, she turned to face her accuser. There stood Betsy with Wyatt

Sullivan, the most popular boy in school, right beside her. Betsy's blonde pigtails, tied back with perfect pink ribbons, shone in the sun. Her dress was no less perfect, pink with just the right amount of lace and even a slight puff to the sleeves.

"Do what, pray tell?" Katherine shot back. Her heart beat furiously in her chest.

"Go down through the mine shaft." Betsy folded her arms in front of her chest and raised an eyebrow.

Katherine's heart skipped a beat then, but she tried not to show her fear.

Ellie Mae's grip tightened on her hand.

"I assure you, Miss Callaway, it's not that I can't do it. It's simply that I have better things to do than to be traipsing about a mine shaft." She turned to leave and hoped that would be enough to silence Betsy.

"Prove it." Betsy's voice rang out after her.

Katherine's eyes slid closed. Was there any way around this? "I have nothing to prove to you," she called back over her shoulder.

"Fraidycat!" Betsy laughed.

The other students joined in.

Katherine's face burned. A fire had been lit within her. She was not afraid of anything! Releasing Ellie Mae's hand, she then whirled around. "I am not afraid!"

"There's only one way we'll believe that." Betsy's hands moved from her chest to her hips.

There was no way this would be a one-way challenge. "Are you going?" Katherine poked her chin out, putting her own hands on her hips, attempting to puff up her chest as much as she could.

"Of course," Betsy said, though her voice caught.

"Then, let's go." Katherine grabbed after Ellie Mae's hand and headed out in the direction of the old mine shaft. She hoped Ellie Mae didn't feel how her palms had started to sweat. Perspiration covered her whole body. How was she to keep up this façade?

The group of students followed, a din of voices behind. As they neared the cavernous opening, they became quiet as they halted several feet short of the forbidden place.

Wyatt pushed through the crowd once they had stopped. "Now, girls, this is foolishness. Talking about it is one thing, but you're not actually going down there, are you?"

Katherine glanced at the mine opening. It looked dark and ominous. Not what she wanted to see. Then she eyed Betsy. She had everything— the popularity, the most handsome boy in school ... But she would not have Katherine's pride, too. "I am."

"Then I am, too." Betsy stared at Katherine, matching her glare through slitted eyes.

"Kath-rine," Ellie whispered, tugging on her hand.

Katherine looked over at her friend. Ellie's eyes begged her not to go. Katherine wondered again at the danger. Her friend had every right to be concerned, she supposed. But it would not last. Betsy would go but a few steps in and give up. Katherine was sure of it. So, she would not be dissuaded.

Wyatt's eyes moved from one girl to the other. A couple of years older than the girls at their thirteen years, he stood a good head taller than Katherine. At last, he threw his hands up in the air. "Then I'm going too."

"And so am I," came Ellie Mae's quiet response.

Katherine leaned toward her friend. "Ellie, you don't have to go." Her eyes held Ellie's. What was she going to do? She couldn't take Ellie into that place. But something had eased in her when Ellie Mae volunteered to go. Was it selfish of her to want her friend to accompany her?

"Yes, I do." Her voice was firm, though her chin quivered. "I'm sticking with you."

A bump in the trail jolted Katherine from her reverie. The scenery outside became blurred. Or was it her? Touching her face, she felt moisture. She wiped at the tears. This would not do! Whatever happened when she returned, Katherine was determined she would face it with as much bravery as she could muster.

To read more, find *Hope in Cripple Creek* here:

https://saraturnquist.com/hope-in-cripple-creek/

Faith in Cripple Creek (Book 3)

Jane Millington has come to Cripple Creek to visit her friend. But a few bumps along the way land her face to face with a man who would rather not become entangled. Not that Jane is looking for a relationship.

Saddened to find her friend struggling after the birth of her child, can Jane offer the hope that she needs?

Timothy Johnson still lives with the sting of betrayal. And he is determined to never risk his heart again. But a chance encounter with a woman who is only passing through leaves him curious.

Can Jane and Timothy offer healing the other so desperately needs?
Will they be able to see beyond past hurts, lean into faith, and find love?

Love in Cripple Creek (Book 4)

A woman burned by love. A man who has lost his way.

Betsy Callaway hasn't been the most upstanding person in Cripple Creek...and she has now passed the acceptable age for marriage. But something about her calls to Nikolai "Nick" Hammond's heart and draws him back home.

The antics that ensue between the pair and the obstacles they face--including their own stubbornness and becoming entangled in a bank robbery-- threaten to keep them on separate paths, but their draw to each other pushes them together.

Will the prodigal find home welcoming?
Can Betsy hope for real redemption?

And the other prequel...

Leaving Stoneybrook

In the rugged terrains of Cripple Creek, David Matthews' world has always been overshadowed by his father. Each sunrise over Stoneybrook Ranch reminds him of the path laid out before him—a life scripted by expectations he isn't sure he can live up to.

Mary Foster has held a silent affection for David since their youth. And while her mother suffers the ravages of a disease they fight to contain, Mary's heart patiently beats in the hope that when David finds his place in the world, there might be room in it for her.

**Will their paths diverge in the vast expanse of the frontier?
Or perhaps love can guide them to find in each other the very thing
they are lacking in themselves—home.**

Acknowledgments

There are some amazing people who continue to make this journey possible. And there are so many people in my life who contribute in so many ways. It is just not possible to thank everyone who touches my life. But I want to take a moment and acknowledge the people whose contributions had a more direct impact on this book.

I want to thank my mentor and editor for this venture, Hannah Conway. Thank you for your insight and input. As always, you keep me honest. My husband weathered a lot of writing hours and feedback sessions over this novella.

Rachel Bull, thanks for using your skills as a photographer to make my hair appear intentional.

For my sister, you make me want to be better. For my parents, you make me feel so good to have achieved this dream of writing. And for my husband and kids, you give me every reason to smile.

Sara is a coffee lovin', word slinging, Historical Romance author whose super power is converting caffeine into novels. She loves those odd little tidbits of history that are stranger than fiction. That's what inspires her. Well, that and a good love story.

But of all the love stories she knows, hers is her favorite. She lives happily with her own Prince Charming and their gaggle of minions. Three to be exact. They sure know how to distract a writer! But, alas, the stories must be written, even if it must happen in the wee hours of the morning.

Sara is an avid reader and enjoys reading and writing clean Historical Romance when she's not traveling.

Please follow along with her journey through her newsletter at: http://saraturnquist.com/list

Also by Sara R. Turnquist

CONVENIENT RISK SERIES

A Convenient Risk

An Inconvenient Christmas

A Less Convenient Path

A Convenient Escape

An Inconvenient Acquaintance

These Golden Years

A Less Convenient Arrangement

Ranch Hands Collection (ebook only)

LADY OF BOHEMIA SERIES

The Lady Bornekova

The Lady and the Hussites

The Lady and Her Champion

The Lady and Her Secret

RAILWAY ROMANCE SERIES

Laura, The Tycoon's Daughter

ACROSS THE YEARS SERIES

Among the Pages

Between the Lines

STANDALONE NOVELS

The General's Wife

Trail of Fears

Off to War

www.ingramcontent.com/pod-product-compliance
Lightning Source LLC
Chambersburg PA
CBHW031445200726
48289CB00008BA/2626